Turning to him, Kat smiled. "I have to go. See you tonight?"

He didn't budge. And then, before he could consider the impact, he said, "Only if you let me restore the boat free of charge, but with one condition."

Slowly, her eyes seized his. "I will not sleep with you, Dane."

A jolt hit his gut at the image of her warming his bed.

Maybe not today. He smiled grimly.

"Wouldn't think of it."

Liar!

Dear Reader,

I invite you into the life of Kat O'Brien, the third sister in my HOME TO FIREWOOD ISLAND miniseries. In *The Doctor's Surprise Family,* Kat perseveres no matter what life tosses out. Suddenly, however, she is falling for a wounded serviceman full of sorrow and secrets whose only goal is to hide from the world. It seems, then, these two are polar opposites…. But Kat will not give up! She is determined to coax this war hero toward a future filled with family and love.

For further details of the first two books of my HOME TO FIREWOOD ISLAND miniseries— *Their Secret Child* plus *And Baby Makes Four*— join me at www.MaryJForbes.com.

Warmest wishes,

Mary

P.S. While *The Doctor's Surprise Family* only hints at a possible experience of war, my greatest hope is that all who serve their country find peace and love waiting at home.

THE DOCTOR'S
SURPRISE FAMILY

MARY J. FORBES

SPECIAL EDITION®

Published by Silhouette Books

America's Publisher of Contemporary Romance

SILHOUETTE BOOKS

Recycling programs
for this product may
not exist in your area.

ISBN-13: 978-0-373-65456-7
ISBN-10:   0-373-65456-1

THE DOCTOR'S SURPRISE FAMILY

Copyright © 2009 by Mary J. Forbes

Visit Silhouette Books at www.eHarlequin.com

Printed in U.S.A.

MARY J. FORBES

Her rural prairie roots granted Mary J. Forbes a deep love of nature and small towns, a love that's often reflected in the settings of her books. Today, she lives with her family in the Pacific Northwest where she also teaches school, nurtures her garden and walks or jogs in any weather. Readers can contact Mary at www.maryjforbes.com.

For A, E and S—
Treasures of our hearts

Chapter One

How long are you going to sit on that motorcycle, pal?

Peering through the rain-splattered front window of her big, rectangular kitchen, Kat O'Brien wondered if the guy even breathed. At least fifteen minutes had gone by and he hadn't moved. Not a muscle, not a gloved fingertip. No, draped in a yellow slicker, he sat still as a stone carving on the leather seat of the big black bike parked in her circular driveway...staring ahead at the surrounding evergreens, leafless birch and maples and verdant winter undergrowth. Perhaps the hammering February sleet had frozen his body in place and it merely waited for a gust of wind to topple it and the bike to the ground.

God forbid, Kat thought.

Well, she couldn't stand here all afternoon ogling the fellow. If he'd come as a potential guest to her bed-and-breakfast, he'd knock on the door when he was ready.

Or if he had gotten lost, sooner or later he'd crank the machine and boot it back to the village proper, a mile up Shore Road.

Restless, she returned to making cookies on the large wooden worktable, the one her late husband had constructed when he was alive, when his big laugh and voice boomed throughout the Victorian he inherited from his grandparents before he married Kat.

Again, she glanced toward the window. Seldom was she leery about her guests, and those she instinctively had gut-twinges about, she didn't book. However, the majority of her customers were annual returnees, folks loving the peace and quiet, the bit of wilderness offered within the hills and forests of Firewood Island. But this stranger had driven slowly up the lane to park and stare at God-knew-what.

Come on, mister, she thought for the tenth time. *Make up your mind.*

A shiver scurried along her arms. She told herself if his intentions were unsavory, he would not have ridden up on a guttural Harley-Davidson. Yet, she wasn't a fool. She always kept her doors locked, and she never questioned her instincts.

Currently, both her rental cabins stood empty. It was, after all, the last Tuesday of February. With fewer vacationers during the winter season in Washington's Puget Sound, she was thankful that at least one man— Dane Rainhart, who'd been her older sister's boyfriend twenty years ago—had booked the smaller cabin last week. He was due to arrive tomorrow for a three-month sabbatical, though from what Kat didn't know.

After putting the third cookie sheet in the oven, she set a candle centerpiece on the ten-seater rectangular oak table that had been in the O'Brien family for eighty years.

Should she stand on the veranda, yell out to gain the guy's attention? Go tap his shoulder or his wet, glossy helmet?

Pressing her lips together to hold back a chuckle, she pictured her eleven-year-old son, Blake, rapping on the helmet…. *Yo, dude. Anybody home in there?* Good thing school was in session for another hour.

Well, hopefully, before the school bus arrived, the man would come to his senses.

Sighing, she slanted another look toward the country-paned front window. Biker-man hadn't budged. Rain gear and big black boots aside, he had to be chilled to the bone.

"Okay, mister," she muttered. "Enough already."

She checked the oven clock—ten minutes left—and headed for the mudroom to grab her red quilted vest off a hook and the orange umbrella out of the stone crock next to the boot shelf. Striding from the kitchen, Kat hurried across the living room to the front entry.

"Either you come in," she grumbled, stepping outside, "or find yourself another driveway to view."

She slammed the door. Not a muscle moved on his body.

Was he dead?

Certainly, he had to be cold. Heck, he had to be frozen.

The veranda's downspouts gushed water into a pair of stocky wooden barrels. The American flag her late husband, Shaun, had hung when they first opened the B and B, drooped like a drenched sheet from its pole-to-pillar attachment.

Flipping up the umbrella, Kat jogged down the six wide steps and strode toward the motorcycle. Under her shoes the lane's gravel lay slick with sleet, while her umbrella vibrated under the onslaught of snow and rain. Relentless since yesterday, the inclement weather chilled the air and vaporized her breath.

"Hi," she said, approaching the man's right side. "Lost your way?"

For the first time, he stirred, turning his head slowly in her direction. Her breath staggered. His irises were the electric-blue of the summer delphiniums she grew in the corners of the porch steps, and his lashes…the rain had clumped them into long dark spears. At first glance, she assumed he was a California beach-bum—his skin sported a deep bronze color. But looking into his cold eyes, she realized the last place he'd want to be was on some beach.

She lifted her free hand, gathered her wits. "I think you made a wrong turn down my road."

His gaze traveled past her shoulder, to the oval sign next to the flag, the wooden sign she'd painted with a border of ivy and delicate white flowers circling scripted gold lettering that read, The Country Cabin.

"I don't think so." The last word cracked before his eyes settled on her again. "You Kat O'Brien?"

"I am." She offered a smile and tried not to stare at how the slick plastic bill of his helmet caught the rain, trickling water onto his cheek in a jagged line following a scar on his whiskery jaw.

Unhurriedly, he removed the helmet and she saw that his neatly trimmed hair was the tarnished-gold color of a harvested grain field.

"I'm Dane Rainhart." His voice was deep, rough. "I'm a day early."

Kat blinked. *Dane...Rainhart?* When she'd accepted his booking eight days ago, heard his name, a mental picture of a tall, gangly teenager emerged. Seventeen years old, frequenting her mother's house with a bunch of high school kids, looking to hook up with Kat's older sister Lee.

Good grief. When had that boy changed into this man—this hollow-cheeked, *stone-faced* man?

Stepping back, Kat reined in her flustered senses. Once, eons before, she'd had a little crush on her sister's boyfriend.

Little, Kat? Try huge. At night you used to squirm in bed thinking about him. And, all right. Since his call she'd reminisced about those days. *Childhood memories, nothing more. Nothing.*

Dane Rainhart had been a silly schoolgirl fantasy before she grew up, attended college and married the love of her life. Simply put, Rainhart's request to rent one of her cabins meant one thing only: a steady three-month income.

Wrapping herself in a cloak of no nonsense, she said, "Why don't you put your bike in the carport and come inside?" Then she headed around the side of the house, pointed to the empty spot next to her old red Honda Civic and waited as her guest walked the motorcycle into the stall. Watching him kick out the stand while his rain gear covered the cement floor in mini-pools of water, she realized he stood much taller than he had in her memories.

He set the helmet on the bike's seat, tugged off the wet slicker and draped it over the handlebars. From the carport's entrance, Kat had a crystal view. This was the boy—*man*—who, more than two decades before, had gazed at her sister with a yearning equal to Kat's own at thirteen, looking at *him*.

Stripped of the rain gear, he wore a bomber jacket and black leather pants as pliable as bread dough. Did he have any idea how those two garments outlined his shoulders, biceps, thighs…?

Don't look further!

She forced her gaze up, but already the tightening had begun deep in her abdomen, and she recognized its source. Dane Rainhart, her teenaged heartthrob, had grown into a powerful, sexy man.

And she'd been a widow for four years, a widow unable to describe the ache of missing her husband.

The man beside the Harley simply brought that loss home.

Across twenty feet of carport, Dane studied the woman silhouetted in the entryway. Her orange umbrella and red vest threw splashes of vibrant color onto the dreary afternoon. Of average height and with a runner's frame, she could pass for a young girl—until a closer check confirmed the slight swell under the vest and the curve of denim at her hips.

She took a step back into the rain. "Come," she said. "We'll get you registered."

"Is it okay that I'm early?" He had worried the cabin wouldn't be available.

"It's fine." Then, as if she had access to his mind, "Your cabin's ready."

With a nod, he followed her through a side door to the back of the house where a cedar deck extended across half its length. Beyond a sketch of lawn and flower garden were two log cabins sheltered within the forest. The larger one stood to the left. A structure a third its size, which Dane assumed would be his for the next twelve weeks, stood to the right.

He couldn't wait to vanish behind its walls.

At the rear door of the house, the woman collapsed her umbrella, shook off the excess water. The nylon covering gone, he noticed her hair was thick and straight as a mare's mane. Curving an inch below her pale jaw, the dark locks framed her face in the same way wooden ovals once framed his granny's ancestral portraits.

"Don't worry about taking off your boots," she said as they entered a spotless mudroom. "Just wipe your feet on the mat."

After setting the umbrella to dry in a tall crock, she led him into an expansive country kitchen. Immediately, his mouth salivated at the aroma and sight of dozens of cookies cooling on tea towels spread across a green worktable with pots dangling overhead.

"Do you like oatmeal raisin cookies?" she asked, passing by the treats.

"Don't mind 'em." He couldn't recall the last time he'd tasted a homemade cookie. Hell, make that homemade *anything*.

She paused, her brown eyes amused. "Grab a couple, if you want. My son loves them, says they're better than chocolate chip. And that's something coming from a prepubescent boy."

"Thanks." Dane took a cookie between his gloved fingers, savored its scent, then pulled open a panel of his coat and slid the treat into his shirt pocket.

She has a kid. His gaze tracked her to a door opposite the dining area, where she disappeared into another room. *Of course, she does, fool. Why wouldn't she?*

Because the possibility hadn't crossed his mind when he booked the cabin. He'd thought the owner or owners were older, with kids out of home or, at the very youngest, in high school. He hadn't expected the girl-next-door as a landlord, and he sure as hell hadn't expected preteens to live within a baseball pitch of where he'd be setting his boots on a mat.

Speaking of which… He glanced over his shoulder. There hadn't been a single male article—boots or shoes, coat or ballcap, fishing pole or golf club—in that mudroom. All Dane saw were a couple of smaller jackets and a pink pair of those rubbery shoes women wore to garden.

Was she separated? Divorced? Widowed?

Why do you give a damn, Dane? You're here to hide and lick your wounds, remember?

She stuck her head around the doorjamb. "Dane?"

Ignoring her familiar use of his name, he crossed the kitchen and entered a small neat office with a beat-up desk, two metal filing cabinets and a window viewing the circular driveway. Posters of her cabins and the main house, along with maps of the village of Burnt Bend and Firewood Island, decorated one wall. His gaze fell to a photo on her desk of a barrel-chested man in a fisherman's hat, laughing at the camera, bear paw hand resting on the shoulder of a tow-haired preschooler. Husband and son?

Behind the desk, Kat O'Brien smiled. "You don't remember me, do you?"

"Should I?" And then, because he'd grown up on the island, he added, "Did we go to school together?"

"I'm Lee Tait's sister. You used to come to my mother's house when you were in high school."

Dane studied the woman across the desk, his

memories scrambling back and back. And then it hit. Except…this woman couldn't be the dark-eyed sprite once nagging her sister to be included in their group. Could she? "You're… Kaitlin?"

"Kat," she corrected. "When I turned sixteen, I wanted a name that sounded fun, so I resigned Kaitlin to the…" her fingers made air quotes "…official drawer."

When he said nothing, when he could only stare, her smile slipped. Setting a pen on the registration book, she said, "I'll also need to include your driver's license on your registration form. Then I'll show you the cabin."

He felt those keen eyes observe his gloved hands as he wrote. Forcing himself to keep his head down, to not blurt, *Be thankful you can't see the scars,* he focused on his breathing. In his peripheral vision, he saw her turn momentarily to one of the metal cabinets.

"Your key," she said handing it over the instant he completed the information. Then, chin up, spine stiff, she led him out the door. "If you choose to eat with us," she said, locking up the office, "breakfast is at eight a.m. each morning, except Sunday when it's at nine. Lunch and dinner are your responsibility. However, I will set out refreshments and snacks at four p.m. on the dinner table." She nodded to the dining section where a long table, stationed in front of a wall-size, country-paned window, faced the circular drive. "You're also welcome to use the guest living room, back deck or sit on the porch gliders. The rest of the house is off-limits."

"Does the cabin have a kitchen?" he asked. Standing in her kitchen with its floor to ceiling cupboards, he noted the bow of her mouth, the way it tilted at the corners as though anticipating that fun she mentioned.

"Yes, both cabins are fully outfitted."

He glanced at her commercial Sub-Zero refrigerator, imagined the food inside, the ten summer guests seated around her table, chatting, laughing, asking each other questions. Though a stab of guilt pierced him, he was infinitely glad the current cold temperatures would give him an excuse to stay in the cottage and refrain from her listed amenities.

He headed for the mudroom, intent on leaving for the privacy of his cabin.

She followed. "I'll show you the way."

Before he could say, *I know where it is. I booked the smaller cabin, remember?* she zipped past him, grabbed the umbrella and was out the back door, her baked cookie scent swirling in his lungs.

Dane stepped onto the deck. Thankfully, a wet gust of wind eradicated her from his nostrils and he inhaled deep to ensure no trace remained. He did not want her image branded into his brain.

Yet he trailed her and that silly umbrella across the strip of wet lawn, up a flagstone path, to the log building sporting another rain-drenched flag, although smaller than the one welcoming visitors onto the veranda of *her* house.

Kaitlin O'Brien was a patriot.

He couldn't get inside the safety of the cabin fast enough.

Before he heard it all again. The roar of the improvised explosive device, an IED. The shattering glass. The deafening blast ripping metal, wood—*bodies*—into a trillion bits.

Before he heard Zaakir's screams, saw the flames destroying—

Stumbling on the first step leading up to the porch, Dane grabbed the newel post. The familiar knot in his throat had him swallowing. *Not now. Not while she's watching.*

"Dane?" She hurried back down the stairs. "You okay?"

"Must've slipped," he lied.

She looked at the step he'd stubbed with his toe. "I'll have someone put down some new weather stripping right away."

Ashamed of his deception, he shook his head and took the steps two at a time. "No need. I'm just tired, is all." Half turning, he looked back. She stayed on the stairs, her fine dark brows puzzled, the rain a wet curtain around her and the pumpkin umbrella. "It's okay," he assured. "And thank you for letting me in a day early." He inserted the key, opened the door.

Guilt pressed hard, crushing his chest. Still, the upbringing he'd had before he'd left the island for the military had him hesitating. He nodded politely. "Goodbye, Kaitlin."

"I'm not going anywhere."

He studied her for a moment. He should explain. He should tell her he was a loner. That life had changed him, Iraq had changed him, war had made him see things in ways she would never understand. He should present some guarantee he wasn't completely crazy. To ease the uncertainty in her eyes.

You don't need to fear me, he wanted to say. *I'm not one of those types.*

She hoisted the umbrella higher, took the lower step. "If you need anything…"

"I know where to find you."

She offered a smile. "Enjoy your stay."

As he watched her walk through the drenched woods, he wondered what she'd say if he told her *joy* was no longer part of his vocabulary.

Chapter Two

Two days later, the Do Not Disturb sign remained on the exterior doorknob of Dane Rainhart's cabin.

Kat could see her commercial yellow-and-white notice from the corner window by the enamel sink where she scrubbed egg from her son's plate. She had walked Blake to the end of her wooded lane ten minutes ago, then returned home the moment they heard the school bus rumbling along Shore Road.

Since his tenth birthday, Blake no longer appreciated his mother waiting in full view of the other bussed kids. Yet, he hadn't wanted to let go entirely of their ritual. Thus, they waited in the lane's bend, and when the bus approached, Kat turned back, out of sight. Sometimes, she caught herself blinking to dispel the sting of tears; soon even this small daily routine would disappear forever.

Nothing stays the same, she thought.

Boys grew into young men.

Husbands died before their time.

And former childhood infatuations became grim-faced loners.

The dishwasher loaded, she made a decision. This morning, she would knock on his door. Whether or not he welcomed the intrusion, she needed to change his bedsheets. Her guest rooms never went a day without clean bedding and a thorough sanitizing, but she had respected his privacy for two days because of the sign, because his motorcycle hadn't moved out of the carport.

However, the time to freshen up the cabin was at hand. Yes, he'd signed on for three months, but that didn't mean she would disregard her business. Sign or not, she'd give the place a scrubbing.

As she tidied her own house and worked in her office, she prepared herself mentally.

He's not the same as he was twenty years ago.

Neither are you, Kat.

At ten o'clock, she gathered sheets, towels, washcloths and two new soap bars from the storage room into a laundry basket. Slipping into her tall, green farm boots, she took a deep breath and stepped out onto the deck.

The air smelled of wet earth and rotted leaves. Gray clouds flecked the sky, though a mellow sun crept among the barren branches. Somewhere, a squirrel chattered and higher up the slope a crow cawed.

The cabin looked lifeless.

She strode up its stone path.

At the porch steps, she faltered. What *had* occupied him for two days, in four hundred square feet of floor space?

Not your concern. Pressing her lips together, she

knocked on the door. And waited. Fifteen seconds, thirty. Another knock, louder this time. Fifteen more seconds.

She was about to lift her hand a third time when the door cracked open. Shadowed in the dim interior and the porch roof, he appeared grimmer than he had getting drenched on his Harley.

"Good morning," Kat said with forced cheer. *Mercy.* The man's potency hit like a hammer. The way he stood there, dressed in all black…sweatshirt, cargo pants, socks…

Tongue-tied, she nudged the basket higher.

His gaze dipped. "Thanks, but I do my own house-keeping."

"The rental price *includes* housekeeping." When he didn't slam the door shut, she took heart. "I'll be no more than ten minutes, and I won't be in your way." When he continued to block her access, she drew a long breath. "Look—why don't I leave these with you? When you're done, leave the dirty laundry in the basket on the porch and I'll pick it up later. And, oh," she nodded to the round flowered tin atop the clean linens, "the cookies are fresh and a bonus."

A glance, then his eyes lifted to her. An electric jolt hit Kat's abdomen. *Smarten up,* she told herself. *You're not a teenager anymore and neither is he.*

With gloved hands, he reached for the bundle in her arms. "Thanks."

Kat frowned. Gloves inside the house? "Is the heater not working?" Darn it, she did not need an added expense this time of year. "If there's a problem with it—"

"The heater's fine. Thanks for the linens and the cookies."

He moved to close the door.

"Is there anything you need me to—"

"No." The doorway narrowed to a slit. "You've done enough, Ms. O'Brien." And then she was alone again.

Kat shook her head. What an odd sort he'd become.

Several seconds passed. No sound came from within. Even the forest had gone silent. She went down the path to her house.

He wore gloves. And black clothes.

A chill skittered across her skin. Was he into drugs? Was he a thief, a mobster on the run? Why wasn't he staying with his parents on the other side of the island? Or at his sister's apartment in the village?

Dozens of possibilities rushed through Kat's mind—and none felt right. Behind that severe Clive Owen facade, Dane Rainhart exuded a soul-deep sadness. His eyes spoke of it whenever he thought she wasn't paying attention.

At her own door, Kat paused. Through the trees, the cabin appeared the cozy getaway she'd always envisioned. Today, the structure resembled isolation and loneliness, two impressions she recognized better than any since Shaun's death.

She went inside to continue her day, but her thoughts journeyed a thousand times to the cabin in the woods.

What made Dane Rainhart so unhappy? And why did she care?

And then there were the hot twinges deep in her core—those she didn't understand at all.

Not when she still dreamed of her late husband.

The following Tuesday morning, the privacy sign no longer hung on the cabin's doorknob. Did that mean he wasn't home? Or was it a message for her to visit?

Twice in the past week, she had exchanged his soiled

bedding for a laundered stack, hoping at the same time to catch a glimpse of him. So far, nada.

Emboldened by the sign's absence, she tugged on a ratty blue cardigan hanging at the back door, and headed out.

Purple crocuses, daffodils and a medley of tulips—characteristic of Puget Sound's mild winters—colored the dark, damp flowerbeds bordering her tiny backyard. On a whim, Kat hurried back into the mudroom and grabbed a pair of pruning shears she kept handy.

She cut a handful of waxy-leafed flowers before slipping the shears into the cardigan's deep pocket and walking to the cabin. The day had dawned bright and clear, the temperature hovering around fifty-eight. March was entering like a lamb.

She knocked twice.

The door remained closed.

Her face warmed. What was she doing, bringing a man flowers, for God's sake? Maybe he had allergies. Or hated flowers.

Before she could change her mind, she tried the knob. The door fell open several inches.

"Hello?" she called softly. "It's me...Kat. I've brought you something..." No answer. "Dane?"

She nudged the door with a fingertip. The cabin lay empty. Crossing the threshold, she paused on the welcome mat to scan the great room/kitchenette.

Her guest was a neatnik. No shirt or jacket draped the jungle-green loveseat or the pair of big-cushioned chairs. No socks hid under the round coffee table in front of the river-rock fireplace. Beside her on the mat, footwear marched in military sync: the harness boots he'd worn on the bike, a pair of loafers and a pair of worn gray slippers.

Intrigued, she stepped out of her rubber boots. Didn't bikers leave cigarette butts and beer cans, girlie magazines and hunting brochures all over? Shouldn't clothes be strewn haphazardly across the furniture?

Why, Kat? Because Shaun used to toss his clothes around the house? A habit you hated, until that terrible moment when you'd give anything to have it back?

She scanned the rooms a second time. Tidy, neat. Everything had its place.

On the knotted-rag rug near the sofa, two big stones—where had they come from?—supported an array of books. Moving closer, Kat read titles on hiking, computers, philosophy and…. She tipped the lone magazine from its slot. *Journal of the American Medical Association?*

Something niggled in her mind. Something Lee mentioned years ago… Yes, that was it… Dane Rainhart had joined the service as a doctor. Kat hadn't kept track; by then she'd been married.

"Can I help you?"

At the sound of his deep voice, she jumped on the spot. "Oh!" Spinning, she pressed her hand against her throat where her heart bounded like a deer in hunting season.

He stood in the doorway, a powerful silhouette against the morning light.

Kat swallowed. "I—I didn't expect you."

"Obviously." Remaining on the threshold, he blocked her flight.

Her gaze darted past his shoulders, to the freedom of the outside world. What did she really know about this man? He'd rented her cabin, yet hadn't welcomed her attempt at housekeeping. In reality, he could be a man hiding from the law, a killer on the loose.

Yes, she had known him more than twenty years ago, but people change. Life alters. *For better and worse.*

Shaun's death proved that.

Looking at Dane Rainhart, she suspected he'd experienced worse as well. Had it changed him? Ignited anger? Prompted a vendetta mission?

Sadness, definitely. She recognized the emotion the moment he looked at her six days ago, amidst snow and rain.

Latching onto that recognition, she thrust out the flowers. "Something from my garden." When he continued to bar the doorway, she babbled on. "If you'd like, I could put them in a glass… On second thought," she tried to smile, "why don't I set them on the coffee table and let you deal with them however you wish." She laid the bundle down. "Okay, then. I'll just get out of your way." Avoiding eye contact, she barreled toward the door. One way or another, he would have to move.

"Kaitlin."

She stood close enough that if he wanted he could reach out—

"I'm sorry I intruded, Dane. It won't happen again." Then with a force that surprised her, "Please, let me pass." Come hell or high water, she was getting out of this cabin.

"Don't be afraid," he said quietly. "I won't hurt you."

Within his space, she could finally see his face, those indigo eyes full of regret, that shockingly sensuous mouth. He'd been where the wind danced in his hair; locks tufted at his hairline and along the crown of his head. "Who said I'm afraid?" she asked.

A smile quirked. "It's all over your face. Sometimes my height can intimidate."

She folded her arms against her stomach. As a teenager, he'd been lean and wiry. At thirty-eight, he carried twenty extra pounds of muscle and sinew, and towered at least ten inches above Kat. Yet, gut instinct said he wasn't a bad guy.

"Look," he said. "I don't know anything about flowers, but I'd hate for that nice bunch," he nodded to the coffee table, "to wilt before the day is done. Would you show me what to do?"

Again his mouth tweaked, and a tremor of heat shot through her. What would it be like to have him kiss—

Lord, what was the matter with her? Turning on her heel, she hurried over, snatched up the bouquet and went to the kitchen sink. When he closed the door and removed his hiking boots, she pictured him setting the footwear on the mat, then slipping on the comfortable slippers.

She reached into the cupboard she'd stocked with chinaware, drew out a tall drinking glass, and filled the container with warm water.

"They're very pretty." He peered over her shoulder, igniting nerve endings she hadn't realized she possessed.

Her fingers fumbled with the stems as she inserted them into the glass. Water sloshed onto the counter. She said, "You need to trim the ends each day and give them fresh warm water."

"Trim the ends?"

"Yes. With a pair of scissors or a knife."

She glanced over. He leaned against the counter, arms crossed. The fact he had yet to remove his gloves puzzled rather than worried Kat. Was it possible he had an aversion to germs, or psoriasis?

She stepped toward the utility drawer next to his hip—and saw the knife sheathed on his belt.

Whoa. How had she missed *that?* Eight inches in length, the thing was a dragon slayer.

Her gaze snapped to his. "Do you always carry knives?"

His irises darkened. "Only when I go into the wilderness."

"Wilderness?" She glanced toward the window and the wooded hills on her five-acre property. "Dane, have you forgotten this island has an area of only twenty square miles? We have chipmunks, squirrels and coyotes. And some deer. Firewood is not the Rockies, Alaska or the Everglades."

"No," he said quietly. "I haven't forgotten what's on this island."

Their eyes held. And again she felt something primal sizzle between them, a lightning she had never experienced.

Catching the tang of the outdoors emanating from his green flannel shirt, she took in the mud-stained hiking boots positioned at the door, before she sized up his black cargo pants. Specks of mud and grass clung to his shins. Where *had* he gone?

"Kaitlin?"

Her head jerked.

A jagged dimple materialized above his scarred jaw. "The flowers?" Amusement lingering in his eyes, he opened the drawer, dug out a pair of scissors, then laid the instrument gently on the counter next to her posies.

Kat released an uneven breath. "Okay," she began. "Each day you snip off the ends." Demonstrating, she cut a half-inch off a tulip stem. "With fresh water, they should last five to seven days, depending on where you place them and the temperature of the cabin."

God, how she could babble.

"How about the eating nook?" He nodded to the booth alcove separating kitchenette from living room. "It gets the morning sun."

She imagined him drinking his first coffee of the day there, perhaps reading one of his magazines or books. She imagined him glancing at the blooms. Thinking of her.

"I'll leave the decision to you," she said, heading to the door. When had a man's proximity jumbled her senses to the point of making her jittery as a silly school-girl? *Not since you were a schoolgirl, Kat, and he was mooning over Lee*.

"Who owns the property with the boatshed and fish shack down by the shoreline?"

The question slammed her to a stop. "That's… They were my husband's. He ran a small fishing business. Salmon, mostly."

Dane remained against the counter. Eyes locked on her, he waited. Kat pushed at her shaggy bangs. "He—Shaun drowned four years ago."

Across the room, the man dwarfing the kitchenette stayed silent. Suddenly she was grateful for that silence, appreciated the way he allowed her to tell what she wanted, when she wanted.

She shoved into her clogs. "In case you're wondering, the boat inside the shed didn't cause his death." Turning for the door, she added, "If you need anything…"

"I'll call."

Of course, he wouldn't, but she lifted a quick hand anyway. "Bye." Pushing open the door, she nearly stumbled into her mother on the other side.

"Goodness, Kat, get hold of yourself." Charmaine Wilson tugged the hem of her mocha-hued jacket straight.

"Mom. What are you doing here?"

The older woman's gaze landed on the man behind Kat. "I might ask you the same thing," she countered.

"Can I help?" Dane stepped onto the porch.

"No," Kat blurted, then flushed with embarrassment. "Everything's fine. Mom, do you remember Dane Rainhart? He was Lee's... One of her school friends."

Charmaine's pupils pinpointed. "'Course, I remember. You've grown up some, Dane."

Before he could respond, Kat snatched her mother's arm and ushered her from the porch. "Why are you here?" she whispered.

Charmaine had a knack of showing up at the most awkward times. Yes, she'd retired from the hair salon, but that did not mean Kat was free whenever her mother had nothing to do. And this morning... Well. "I thought you were babysitting for Addie today." Kat's youngest sister had an eight-month-old son whom Charmaine cared for while Addie taught math part-time at Fire High.

"Alexander has a little cold," the older woman explained, "so your sister called in a sub. Which brings us to why I'm here. I brought Blake home."

Kat's adrenaline spiked. "Why? Is he sick?"

"Seems he has the same bug as Alex."

"Why didn't the school call?"

"They did, but you weren't answering."

No, *she* was busy with her guest. Kat walked to the house.

In the comfort of her kitchen she called, "Blake?"

"Here," came the hoarse reply from upstairs.

She hurried up the stairwell, down the hallway, to the first bedroom on the left. Her son lay on his side on top of the quilt.

"Hey, honey." She walked over, sat on the bed,

brushed a dark curly lock—so like his father's—from his forehead. "Grams said you weren't feeling well."

"Throat hurts. The school said you weren't home." Accusation pinched the words.

"I was housekeeping at the cabin." Warmth struck her skin. *Liar. You were trying to get Dane Rainhart's attention.*

From the pillow, Blake gave her a one-eyed stare. "Thought the guy didn't want housekeeping."

As always, she had informed him about their guest. "The sign was down today."

"Oh."

Kat hated seeing her child in discomfort. "Want some chicken soup?"

"'Kay."

Rising, she removed his sneakers, then tugged his pajamas from under the pillow. "Get into these and I'll be back with the soup."

She was almost at the door when he asked, "Is that guy staying here forever?" Blake rose into a sitting position, feet on the floor. Over the course of the last year he'd grown to equal her height.

"No," she said, "just until June first."

"I saw him sneaking around in the forest last Friday."

"Sneaking around?"

"Yeah, like he was creeping up on something. He had on one of those army coats like you see on the news? And these big boots like Dad used to wear—you know, with the laces? Anyway, it looked like he was playing G.I. Joe or something."

Kat frowned. Not thirty minutes ago, Dane had stood in the doorway of the cabin dressed exactly as Blake described. With a hunting knife strapped to his waist.

And he'd arrived without a sound.

She forced a smile. "Grown men don't play G.I. Joe, Blake."

"This one does," he said hoarsely.

Pushing aside this morning's imposing image, Kat advised, "Get under the covers and stay warm. I'll be right back."

Downstairs, Charmaine stirred a pot of chicken broth at the stove. She said, "I stopped at my place for some homemade."

"Thanks." Already the comforting scent of soup suffused the room. Kat prepared a tray. Beyond the corner window above the sink, bits of the cabin peeked through the leafless trees. The porch was once again empty, the door firmly shut, the sign in place.

Charmaine glanced over. "He stayed outside for a long time, you know."

She didn't have to ask who.

"Looked like one of those plantation overseers you read about in history books, standing on the porch, arms crossed, feet planted. Gave me the willies the way he stared straight at the house."

"He's probably interested in people from his past," Kat said, recalling her own endless curiosity concerning the man who was her father, the man whose name Charmaine refused to disclose—no matter how much Kat begged, cajoled and argued. She tamped back her bitterness with a sigh. The disagreement would go on forever. "Anyway, it's been years since he's been on the island."

"Well," Charmaine continued, "why isn't he staying with his family? His parents must be wondering, and his sister, too."

The senior Rainharts worked at the Burnt Bend Medical Clinic, their daughter was the local social worker.

"Why is he hiding out here?" Charmaine asked.

Hiding out. Was that it? Kat wondered as the office telephone rang. Grateful for an excuse to escape her mother, she hurried to pick up the receiver. "Country Cabin, Kat O'Brien speaking."

"Is the boy all right, Kaitlin?"

Dane. Her breath caught. "He's fine," she said, wariness surfacing. "How did you…?"

"I saw your mother pick him up from the elementary school when I was on the trail across the road."

The eight-mile hiking trail circling forest and parkland and, at one point, paralleling the school grounds. The trail Blake mentioned two minutes ago. "I see."

"I needed to clear my head. Walking helps." Pause. "Is there anything I can do?"

You can stop making me wonder about you. "No," she said. "But thanks for asking."

After hanging up, she sank into her desk chair. Now what? Both her son and her mother questioned Dane's motives. Still, intuition told Kat different. He'd erected an invisible wall, one, she suspected, that shielded his pain from the world. After Shaun died, she'd erected a similar barricade. So. Should she ask Dane to leave— or let him stay?

She was still weighing her options when a knock sounded on the mudroom door.

Charmaine frowned as Kat walked through the kitchen, nerves jittery at the prospect of seeing *him* again. But when she opened the door, no one stood on the back deck and the morning sun remained as bright as it had fifteen minutes earlier.

She looked toward the cabin, hoping to see something, anything, but all remained silent amidst the forest. Where had he gone—and so fast?

Forget him, Kat. Right now Blake needs you.

She was about to shut the door when a folded notebook page tucked under a corner of the outside mat caught her eye. Her heart kicked. Bending slowly, she retrieved the page.

Thanks for the flowers, he'd written in a tall, narrow scrawl. *You've given me a different memory.*

No signature. But then, none was needed.

Kat raised her head, gazed into the woods.

A different memory.

Deep in her soul she knew that it wasn't the flowers, but her.

She was the memory, the difference. And, she sensed, neither held regret. Note secured in her shirt pocket, she turned back into the house wondering if he realized how often she would read his ten words before the day was done.

Chapter Three

The nightmare stampeded into Dane's sleep with a vengeance.

Reaching. He was reaching again. Reaching to no avail, even though his hands closed over thin shoulders, shielded terrified dark eyes. Everywhere hung the stench of smoldering flesh. His own and Zaakir's.

Still, he pretended. Lied. *I'm here. I've got you. Help is coming.* Except, wasn't he the help? Wasn't he the doctor?

He'd arrived too goddamned late. *Again.*

He wrenched upright. Struggled for air. Fought against smoke, against fire. Fought, fought, fought—No. *No.*

He was in bed. In the cabin he'd rented.

Gradually, his grip on the comforter eased. He was okay. It was just a dream.

His heartbeat leveled. The panting abated.

Another damn night shot. Two in the morning and he might as well rise and shine. Three, four hours sleep was his normal now.

Tossing back the quilt, he climbed naked from bed. Cool air struck his hot, damp skin like a blessing. He'd take a walk along the ocean, let the night wind sweep the mess from his brain.

Ten minutes later, dressed in a thick flannel shirt, jeans, army coat and hiking boots, he stepped out onto the cabin's porch.

As always at this hour, the first thing he noticed was the chilly punch of winter and the raw spice of ocean on the breeze, so different from the desert sand. Tonight, no moon or stars cluttered the sky. Instead, he stood surrounded by inky darkness. Beyond the steps, the flagstones vanished into the woods, and above them cut the roofline of the house where Kat and her son slept.

Flicking his flashlight, he went into the forest, found the rough, overgrown trail he had discovered his first evening here. The one meandering down the slope, toward the shoreline and ending at the fish-and-tackle shack and weathered boatshed amidst the conifers. He had wandered around the shed on several occasions, tried the locked double doors at both ends, peered into its three grimy windows.

From his initial inspection that first night, he knew the old fishing trawler or lobster boat was constructed of wood—a beautiful wood, given the right TLC—and might have been built in Maine.

Tonight, he shone his light once more against the gray walls, the deadbolt locks, the windows. Barely visible through the dirty panes, he noted the peeling name on the rear of the boat: *Kat Lady*.

A name her husband conceived? And had she docked the craft after his death?

Dane itched to get inside the building, to assess what could be done to make the vessel viable in the ways his grandfather had taught when Dane was a kid and rode the Sound with the old man. He'd been thinking about scraping and varnishing and remodeling the craft since he'd made his discovery. Three months would get the job done. A perfect time frame.

Okay, his bent was selfish. He couldn't help that. He needed a motive to get up every day, an objective to mull over at night, to dream about—and Kaitlin's old trawler fit the bill.

He didn't need to ask why she had locked the vessel away, why she hadn't sold this part of her late husband's life. Selling, he knew, would mean goodbye...forever. Something he'd had to do in an instant with his medical career, with Zaakir. And then there was his marriage—although that goodbye had happened in stages. Still, the sorrow and regret he'd felt when Phoebe left Iraq to live stateside had sometimes overwhelmed him. He'd let her down in so many ways. Sure, she'd remarried, but that didn't negate the fact *he'd* been a lousy husband.

The briny-scented wind filled his lungs as he skirted the light along the rear window frame. Had he been a less decent man, he would break the pane, reach in, unlatch the window. Except, he wasn't a burglar, or a destroyer of property. He was a healer. Or had been.

Damn it to hell. Quit letting those memories hound you. Quit letting them rule your life.

Wheeling around, he strode past the boatshed and down to the shore where a wooden pier thumbed forty feet into Admiralty Inlet. Against the planks his boots thudded like hollow shots as he walked to the end of the quay. An icy wind whipped drops of seawater against his face. He jacked his collar up to protect his ears. His hands found the carryall pockets of his jacket.

He shouldn't care about her boat. He shouldn't speculate about her reasons for leaving it to decay in that cavernous shed.

Tomorrow he'd knock on her door, ask if he could fix the vessel.

And if she tells you to go to hell?

If the shoe were on the other foot, wouldn't *he* be tempted to tell *her* exactly that?

Restless, Dane strode off the pier and headed for the cluster of boulders a short distance away. Settling on top of the largest rock, he gazed at the night sea tossing its whitecaps ashore.

He tried not to think of the way she'd looked when she brought him that armful of flowers, or why he'd left a note on her doorstep. He tried not to remember Iraq, and the reason he was no longer a doctor. That his hands, his surgeon's hands, were scarred and disfigured from a war which shattered the life he'd worked his guts out to attain. The life—when all was said and done—he'd loved more than his marriage. And he tried not to mull over his own skewed logic for ignoring his parents and sister.

In the end, he thought of them all. And when he finally returned to the cabin, his brain was in a worse muddle than before.

Until he spotted the flash and color of the bouquet on his table and recognized Kat O'Brien as the one quiet element in his mind.

His lifeline.

* * *

Three nights later, he heard the creak of a twig to the right of the porch where he sat in a wicker chair enjoying the evening quiet. Something stole through the forest. Ears straining for the slightest sound, Dane remained motionless, two traits he'd learned in Iraq when darkness closed in and rebels prowled villages, on the hunt for drugs brought along by medical teams.

These days on Firewood Island, night fell around five p.m., obliterating shadows and outlines and things that moved in the trees.

Several silent moments passed. Then…a soft crunch, as though someone stepped on a thick carpet of dead leaves.

Dane's body tensed. Had the person noticed him on the porch?

His gaze zeroed in on the large cabin in the trees across Kaitlin's backyard. Last night, Dane had observed lights in two windows. A second guest? He didn't care, as long as they kept to their side of the property and left him alone.

Without making a sound, he got to his feet—and waited. The rustling had stopped. Creeping down the steps, he went around to the side facing the wooded hill. His eyes narrowed against the forest's obscurity.

Someone panted softly.

Dane stepped into the block of light shining from the window of the eating nook.

"Holy crap," a boy's voice muttered, before the kid scrambled like a wild animal back up the slope.

Dane leaped toward the escapee, entering the trees like a predatory animal, silent, quick. Without a word, he sprang over moldering logs, and ducked grasping branches. Ten feet ahead the kid dodged right and left. Suddenly, he turned and scrambled farther up the hill, and then—abruptly—twenty feet ahead, Dane saw arms, legs and branches whip like miniature windmills. *Thunk.*

"Ow!" the boy yelped. Gasping and wheezing and clutching his leg, he writhed on a wet bed of leaves.

Dane approached slowly.

"Please," the boy whispered. "I didn't mean it."

"Easy, son." Dane frowned at the slashed denim along the boy's left leg. Crouching on one knee, he shrugged from his jacket and laid the garment across the boy's chest. "Got a name?"

"Y-Yes sir. Blake." The winded words came out *Yea seer bake.*

Kaitlin's son?

The wheezing accelerated. Blake's face altered, faded, and for an instant Zaakir stared up at Dane.

He swiped a hand across his eyes. He was losing it, and *this* kid was showing every sign of an asthma attack. "Where's your inhaler, son?"

"Home."

Sure, it was. Damn kid, creeping through the woods in the dark and forgetting his lifeline. Dane squashed the urge to give Blake a good shaking. Instead, he scooped the boy into his arms. "Hang on." Careful of wayward limbs, he trotted through the trees, crossed Kaitlin's back deck and, while the boy clung to his neck, yanked open the mudroom door.

"Inhaler," he hollered, storming into the kitchen with Blake wheezing against his chest. *"Now."*

Kat didn't have time to think or ask questions.

The second Dane set her son next to the plate of

hard-boiled eggs she'd been slicing for the spinach salad on her big worktable, Kat ran to the dining cabinet and grabbed the emergency inhaler.

"Darn it, Blake," she said, shoving the tool into his hands. "What have I told you about keeping this with you at all times?" Heart pounding, she forced herself to watch calmly as he tilted back his head and put the instrument to his mouth. Still, she couldn't help advising, "Breathe deep."

He rolled his eyes.

She released a shaky sigh. Okay. Not as bad as she'd first thought when Dane banged into her house. Already the first healing puff had altered her child's skin from pale and sweaty to pink and dry as added oxygen rushed into his blood.

Relieved, she turned to Dane. He stood in a white T-shirt, dog tags dangling from his neck, gloved hands clutching the end corners of the worktable. His dark eyes were fastened on Blake, his expression harsh. Kat's stomach looped at the man's scrutiny. Had she misread him after all? "What happened?"

"It was my fault," Blake interjected before her guest could reply. "I was trying to look into Mr. Rainhart's window and—and he caught me, and then I ran into the woods and fell and…" When he straightened his leg, she noticed the bloody damage for the first time.

Kat's pulse bounced. "Oh, baby." She bent over the torn skin. Deep and raw, the gash measured about four inches along her son's bony shin.

Removing the desert jacket from Blake, Dane said, "He needs stitches. If you have gauze to wrap the wound, I can ready him for transport to the clinic."

Ready him for transport? Disregarding the odd turn

of phrase, Kat hurried to the cupboard with its stored First Aid supplies. Had Blake told her the truth, or had Dane Rainhart hurt her son somehow, perhaps frightened him into lying?

She nearly dropped the kit when she heard her son whimper. She hurried back as Dane gently straightened Blake's leg. "Looks like that tree root did quite a number on you," he said, inspecting the gash.

From what Kat could see "the tree root" had gouged the flesh just below the knee. Blake puffed his cheeks at the sight of his blood-soaked jeans. "I think I'm gonna be sick."

Dane placed a gloved hand on the back of her son's neck. "Lower your head down toward your knees. That's it." He waited a few moments. "Feeling better?"

"A little." Blake raised his head. "I—I didn't m-mean to spy on you. Honest."

"That what you were doing?" Dane hauled the knife off his belt and Kat's heart lurched—until she saw that he meant to trim away the jagged edges of denim from her son's wound.

Blake gaped while Dane deftly cut a neat rectangular hole. "Kaitlin," he said, "we'll need some warm water, a pinch of mild soap and a washcloth."

She rushed to get the materials. Behind her, Blake murmured, "I—I just wanna be a soldier when I grow up." She couldn't catch Dane's response.

Moments later, she watched as he cleaned Blake's wound with the gentlest of motions, dipping the cloth into the water and touching it around the torn flesh. When it came time to dress the gash he directed her to cut the gauze—*not that way*—bind it around the gash—

to the left—snip the gossamer ends, and knot them correctly.

If he knew first aid, why wouldn't he remove his gloves and do the procedure himself?

Shoving him from her mind, she hunted down her stash of Children's Tylenol.

"Bring your car to the front door," Dane told Kat after she observed her son swallow the painkiller. "I'll carry the boy outside."

"I can walk," Blake assured. He jumped off the worktable onto his good leg and limped from the kitchen.

Two minutes later, Kat locked up the house. Driving down the lane, she caught sight of Dane in the Honda's side mirror. Arms crossed, he stood on the bottom step of her veranda, a formidable, forbidding man watching her leave the property.

What do you really know about him, Kat?

He'd had medical training, that was a given. *Had* he become the military doctor her sister Lee alluded to years ago? Given the desert fatigues he wore, Dane Rainhart had clearly served his country in some capacity.

That being the case, the sadness, the aloofness, the loner attitude seemed to resemble post traumatic stress disorder. Last winter, Lee had pondered the symptoms during her brief relationship with Col. Oliver Coleman before he was killed in action in Iraq.

"You mad at Mr. Rainhart, Mom?" Blake's question from the rear seat jerked Kat away from the memory.

"Not at all. Why?"

Worried brown eyes filled the rearview mirror. "I was scared at first, but then I realized he was only trying to help. He wasn't mean or anything."

"You shouldn't have spied on him, Blake. Looking

through people's windows is an invasion of privacy and very wrong. You know better. What on earth made you do such a thing?"

"I dunno." He hung his head; dark hair fell over his smooth brow. "I'm sorry."

Kat turned out of their wooded lane and onto Shore Road leading into the village of Burnt Bend. "It's Mr. Rainhart you need to apologize to."

"I will," the boy murmured.

The promise did nothing to loosen the knot in Kat's stomach. Her son had never peered into the windows of her guests' cabins. Why did he do so now?

She wondered what Dane thought of Blake. She wondered what he thought of her parenting skills. Then she wondered why his opinion was important enough for her to contemplate. The man was part of her past, not her future. Right now, she needed to concentrate on getting her son medical attention. Beyond that, nothing else mattered.

Yet, the feeling Dane Rainhart wasn't finished with her continued to hover over Kat's shoulder.

He sat on the cabin steps, watching for her headlights to play peek-a-boo through the lane's trees, to tell him she had returned home with the boy. The moment her car disappeared, he'd gone for a hard, fast hike through the hilly forest behind her property.

The kid's chest hadn't been crushed under the weight of metal. The wheezing was the result of asthma.

The knowledge had punctuated Dane's every step. Guided by the flashlight, he'd climbed across mossy stones, through thick undergrowth and dodged gnarly tree limbs until *his* chest heaved, and the whistling sound of her son's condition subsided.

Now he waited. Without light or warmth from the cabin.

He heard the grumble of a motor before headlights trickled through the forest. Seconds later, she pulled into the carport. Doors slammed. Voices, hers and the boy's, drifted softly on the night.

A brick of tension dropped from his body. They were home. The boy was okay. Still, he waited. Waited until the big house lay in darkness, except for an upstairs window.

Suddenly, the narrow, rectangular pane beside the mudroom door lit behind its lacy curtain.

Dane rose from the chair when he heard a latch click. Footsteps crossed the deck. Kaitlin? Or the boy, sneaking out again?

He went down the flagstone path.

She stood on the edge of the deck, wrapped in a pale shawl. Damn, she was lovely, like an elf come out to play under the stars.

"Kaitlin?" he queried softly and saw her body jerk.

"Good heavens, you're a quiet one."

He hadn't meant to startle her. Keeping to the delta of the path, he asked, "How's the boy?"

"Eight stitches. The doctor says he can go to school tomorrow, just no roughhousing on the playground."

Dane nodded.

A handful of seconds passed. She asked, "Are you a military doctor?"

"Not anymore."

"A doctor here, then? You seemed to know exactly what to do with Blake's injury."

He hesitated. "I was a trauma surgeon in Iraq. Served there since we went in. Left a year-and-a-half ago." He'd been in the Middle East almost six years. Too damned long to work in a place where you never knew if your next breath would be your last.

She remained silent, studying him as he studied her. Finally, she said, "I was coming to see you, but your lights were off."

"I like sitting on the porch in the dark. It's peaceful."

"I understand."

He imagined she did. She would need the peace following her husband's death.

She said, "I want to apologize for my son's behavior. It won't happen again."

"He's a typical kid. Don't worry about it."

"Being a kid is no excuse. He'll apologize after school tomorrow."

"All right."

As she turned to go, she paused. "Would you like to join us for dinner tomorrow? As a thank-you for helping Blake tonight."

"Help?" *The way I helped Zaakir?* Dane bit hard on his tongue to sever the memory. "It was my fault he got hurt," he murmured. "If I hadn't chased him—"

"We're all a little to blame," she replied reasonably. "However, if you'd rather not…"

"I'm surprised you'd trust me after tonight."

"Why wouldn't I?" She stepped off the deck and crossed to him. "Dane, I don't know your past, or what's eating you. That's your business. But from what I've seen so far, from what I remember, you're all right. So if you like roast chicken with stuffing, dinner will be at six tomorrow."

He could smell her on the night air, caught himself lifting his chin an inch to better draw in the scent. "You'd be wise to stay away from me," he said.

She smiled. "Perhaps. Except I don't scare easily."

The night trapped them, a thick swathe of darkness in which he could imagine the heat of flesh slipping along flesh. His gaze seized her, beckoned her, told her a thousand stories.

"Be careful, Kaitlin. I'm not the man you remember." Turning on his heel, he walked back into the shroud of night.

Chapter Four

A woodpecker rat-a-tatted somewhere in the pines outside his window. He jerked awake, not because of the bird, but because the sun stood well above the trees and the clock read 9:46 a.m.

He'd slept ten hours straight. When was the last time he'd overslept? Not since college when he'd been studying half the night for a physics exam.

His tangled brain took in the tiny bedroom with its one piece of knotty pine furniture housing his underwear and socks. *Kaitlin.* He was in her cottage.

And, he'd fallen asleep to wake hours later with—he glanced down—the worst arousal he'd had in two decades.

Scraping both hands down his stubbled cheeks, he drew in a sigh, then flung back the downy quilt and set his feet on the rug beside the bed. He needed a shower, a freezing shower.

Naked, he headed down the short hallway to the bathroom.

The kitchen phone rang. Who'd be phoning on the landline? Had to be her.

Down the hall he went and into the kitchen. A glance at the window; no boy peered back at him. Dane picked up the receiver. "Hello?"

"Good morning," she sang.

He cleared his rusty throat. "'Mornin'."

Pause. "Oh, Dane. I woke you, didn't I?" If he'd needed a shower to cool down two minutes ago, that breathless *Oh, Dane* doubled the requirement. "I'm so sorry," she went on. "I'll let you get back to bed."

"No, no. Was up reading," he fibbed. He glanced toward the front door and its half-moon window draped with a frilly curtain that let in the light, but obscured prying eyes. Phone to his ear, he walked over, tried to peer through to the Victorian, and imagined her in that country kitchen with its big worktable.

She said, "I didn't mean to disturb you—"

Just thinking of her disturbed him. "Kaitlin?"

"Yes?"

"Stop apologizing."

Another pause, longer this time. Was she remembering his asinine remark last night? *I'm not the man you remember.* And where the hell had his grouchy tone come from? He'd been raised to respect and honor a woman, to treat her with decency. To do anything less was as foreign to him as giving birth. He just wasn't built that way.

"I wanted to make sure you were still coming to dinner tonight."

So, she had been recalling his words.

He headed for his bathroom. "I'll be there."

"Good. Um… Is there anything you need from town? Anything for your fridge? I'm doing a grocery run in about ten minutes."

"No thanks." The only thing he needed she couldn't give.

"Okay…. I'll see you tonight."

"I'll be there."

He waited for her to hang up. She didn't.

"Aren't you hanging up?" His voice scratched.

This time her hesitation stretched even longer. "Aren't you?" she replied softly.

Oh, hell. What could he say? *I want to hang up but can't? I need to hang up before I grab a pair of jeans and go to your back door?*

Where he'd kiss her the way he wanted to last night—

"I'm looking forward to seeing you again," she whispered into his ear, and pictures of her in the night bloomed across his brain.

"You're all I thought about before I went to sleep," he confessed.

"Me too, you." And then she released a long breath as if coming to a conclusion. "However, I'd rather be friends."

"I'm not interested in a relationship." Not the kind she deserved.

"That's good to know." Relief crept in. "Because it never would have worked. We're too different."

She was right, they were; but that didn't make the truth easier. "Says who?"

"Says me. You're too intense, too…dark."

"Dark?"

"You've got things inside you."

How could she know he had Zaakir inside him?

Zaakir, who was never going to leave, who would haunt Dane until his dying breath.

Except, last night Dane had been free. For ten hours the ever-present guilt had lifted, flown. Until now, until he realized he hadn't thought of the boy since yesterday.

He needed to get off the phone. He couldn't hold her responsible for fixing him, and somehow he knew she'd want to do exactly that if she found out about the darkness that plagued him.

"I'll see you tonight," he repeated, because he had promised. Then he set the phone gently in its cradle.

He no longer needed a cold shower.

He'd been working on the Harley thirty minutes when he sensed Kaitlin's son enter the carport from the backyard. Crouched on a square of cardboard, Dane continued to sweep the battery terminals clean with the small steel brush that was part of his toolkit. Maybe if he ignored the kid, he'd go away again.

"Whatcha doin'?"

No such luck. The boy was here to socialize and Dane wasn't in the mood, and for damn sure not while he was checking out the bike's battery. Already memories of another kid and a different battery surged up; he worked to control his breathing, to pinch back the images.

Blake wandered to the cardboard. His sneakers were scuffed, but what Dane could see of the boy's blue jeans appeared clean. *Go away, son. You could get hurt again.*

"What's the matter with the battery?"

"Needs a checkup." He had yet to look the kid in the eye.

"My mom gets her car checked at the garage in town."

"Good for her."

His tone didn't deter the boy; he squatted on his haunches next to Dane. "Harley-Davidson motorcycles are the best, right?"

That's it, kid. Go for the power, the look, the sound.

Picking up his flashlight, Dane shone the beam against the clear box to check the fluid in each cell. His pulse rate accelerated. Didn't Blake realize battery fluid was acidic, what it could do to your skin? Damn it, didn't they teach anything in school? And where was Kaitlin? Did she know her son was in a place where he could get hurt?

"You need to back up," he told the boy, pointing to a spot at least six feet away.

"Why?"

"Batteries can be dangerous."

"Really? My dad once changed the battery in his pickup and he never said that."

"Ever heard of acid?"

"Uh-huh. We did an experiment in science last fall with acid."

"Know what it can do?"

"Sure. Can I sit on your bike when you're done? I've never sat on a motorcycle before."

As he spoke, the boy moved in the direction Dane had instructed. He breathed easier. "Don't you have something to do?" he grumped. "Like help your mother?"

"Already did. I cleaned my room and collected the trash around the house."

"Well, maybe there's something else you could help her with, something she hasn't thought of."

"Nuh-uh. She said I could go outside 'cause it's not raining. And anyway, I like talking to you." The boy flushed and shot Dane a sheepish grin. "You know…

about the Harley an' stuff. When my dad was alive I was too little to know about motorcycles and anyway he didn't have a Harley."

Was the boy was looking for a stand-in daddy? *Hell.* Knees popping, Dane rose to his full height and gazed down at Kaitlin's son for a long moment, so long the kid's grin faded. One sneaker heel began bouncing up-down, up-down.

Ignoring the flare of sympathy in his chest, Dane said in a rough voice, "This isn't going to work, Blake. I'm the kind of guy who likes his privacy and—"

"I thought I heard voices out here." Kaitlin stepped into the carport, cutting off Dane's next words.

"Mom!" The boy waved her over. "Come see Mr. Rainhart's Harley. Cool, huh?"

"Yes, it is," she replied, eyes on her son. "Did you apologize to Mr. Rainhart yet?"

The boy hung his head. "Oh, yeah. Sorry for looking in your window. It was a really bad thing to do."

Dane stood on the other side of the cardboard square wishing Kaitlin would take her son and leave. Family conferences weren't his thing. Still, he nodded. "No worries." He looked directly at Kaitlin. "Look, I need to finish up here."

His message put a small tight smile on her lips. "Let's go, son. You promised to play with Danny this afternoon, remember?" She darted a look at Dane. "Danny's Blake's eight-year-old cousin."

"Aw… Can't we wait until Mr. R's done fixing the Harley?"

"No," Kaitlin said. "Aunty Lee is expecting you."

"O-kay." Shoulders hunched, feet dragging, Blake left the carport.

Kaitlin's gaze flicked to the Harley. "My son won't bother you again." She turned to leave.

Dane stepped around the battery and was in front of her before she got to the door. "It's not what it seems."

"You don't need to explain, Dane. Kids can be intimidating for someone who's not used to all their questions."

He let his head fall back on a weighty breath before he said, "It's not that. I… I had a bad experience with a child."

A puzzled expression crossed her features. "I don't understand."

His memories battled with the yearning to tell all. The memories won. He would not put the quagmire of his past, of Zaakir's death, on her shoulders. She had enough in her life with an asthmatic son and trying to operate a business without a husband. Still, he couldn't let her walk away without some kind of explanation.

"A child was hurt on my watch," he said.

"And you blame yourself." Her brown eyes, full of commiseration, held his for three thick seconds.

"I need to get back to work." He strode to the motorbike.

"Dane…"

"Go, Kaitlin. Your son is waiting."

When her footsteps ebbed, he crouched at his toolkit and with shaky fingers dug out a wrench. *Concentrate on the bike. Don't think of her. Don't think at all.*

Two hours later, when he took the Harley out on the road, her words trailed him like wisps of a ghost. *You blame yourself.*

Oh, yeah. She was dead-on there.

Carrying a canvas tote filled with fresh produce, Kat walked through the electronic doors of Dalton Foods on the corner of Main and Shore Road. A block up the street, in the library lot, she'd parked her car under the leafless elms. She would make a quick stop, pick up the book Ms. Brookley had called about this morning, then head home to prepare for tonight.

A smile flickered on her lips. She hoped Dane liked baked red potatoes, seasoned with basil and oregano, and shallots and mushrooms in cream sauce. She hoped he liked upside-down pineapple cake. Tonight's dinner would be beyond special, she rationalized, if for no other reason than to create other memories for him, to take away that emptiness she saw so often in his eyes.

"A child died on my watch."

Had the child died on the operating table? Had Dane—

"Kat," a male voice called as she reached the crosswalk to the Burnt Bend Library. "Got a minute?"

She turned to see a stocky man, face shielded by a worn ballcap and a foam cup of coffee in one hand, jog across the street that ran behind the shops edging the boardwalk of the village's tiny cove. Kat recognized him immediately. Colin Dirks, Shaun's cousin, from Bainbridge Island. They hadn't seen each other since Colin's fishing trawler capsized during a sudden squall. Since Shaun drowned in that squall and Colin lived. Kat couldn't help the spurt of anger. He'd been the one to coax Shaun away that weekend.

Oh, initially Colin had offered condolences, but then things changed. His calls and e-mails took another slant. Rather than asking about her and Blake, or talking about the man Colin claimed had been like a brother, he wanted to know when was she going to sell him the *Kat Lady?*

Never, she thought for the hundredth time as she observed him approach with his feigned concern.

"Here with your family, Colin?" she asked, certain he'd come alone to Firewood Island; certain, too, of the reason.

"Nope. They're home. I was just—" he glanced over his shoulder "—getting a mocha at Coffee Sense before I came to see you. But this is even better. Can I buy you a coffee?"

A snarky retort on her lips, she turned. But then she remembered that this man had been Shaun's childhood best friend. It wasn't as if Colin had planned the squall, or the capsizing of his trawler. And Shaun had gone on his own volition that weekend to pitch in when one of Colin's helpers had come down with the flu.

She tried to smile, to keep things light. "Thanks, but I've already had too much coffee." In truth, she'd had one cup and would love another, but not with him. "And I'm in a bit of a hurry. What did you want to talk about?"

He squared his shoulders, jutted his bristly jaw. "Well, if you can't make the time…"

Pointedly, she checked the watch on her wrist. "I'm sorry, I'm already running late."

His eyes probed hers. "All right, then. Let's get to the point. Why won't you sell me the *Kat Lady?* I'll give you top dollar for her. Hell, have you even opened the doors of the shed since Shaun died, Kat? I'll bet you haven't. I'll bet it'll sit there until you're walking with a cane. You think your boy will want the damned thing? Gimme a break. Kid doesn't have the stamina for the sea."

She gaped at the man her husband had likened to a brother. "I think you've overstepped your boundaries, Colin. Please don't mention that boat or my family again." She turned to go. *Ass.*

"That boat," he scoffed, "could bring you a good price, one I'd be willing to pay."

Just as she stepped into the crosswalk, he caught her arm. "What's wrong with you to hang onto a vessel that'll just rot where she sits? Don't you have any respect for Shaun? He'd want her on the water. He wouldn't want her stuck in some building, collecting cobwebs." His voice had risen with each sentence. A woman passing by gave them an odd look. "Don't you get it, Kat? This is not what Shaun would want."

"Let go of me," she said quietly, but with enough steel that he did as she asked. "As to what Shaun wanted, no one knows what my husband wanted more than I do."

Determined to be rid of the man, she walked across the street, her eyes on the library doors. "We are not having this conversation again, Colin. Do you hear?"

He kept astride. "Then sell me the boat. She's no use to you."

Kat stopped on the other side of the street. The library doors were fifteen feet away. "She's everything to me—something you wouldn't understand. All she is to you is a boat to make money."

A bark of laughter. "You think she wasn't that to Shaun?"

"No."

"Hell, he wanted to get rid of her! Do you know what he told me that weekend he went fishing with us?"

She didn't want to hear a bunch of lies.

But Colin Dirks wasn't finished. "He told me he wished you wouldn't have forced him back to the island. He hated it here. He wanted to be the marine biologist he'd dreamed of being since fourth grade. He almost made it, too, until you came along. Sell me the boat and do him a favor."

"A favor? Shaun's dead! Dead, do you hear? Because

he was on *your* boat." Fingers clenching the straps of the grocery tote, Kat worked to steady her breathing. Another word from him and she'd clout him with five pounds of potatoes. "Now, go home to your family and don't ever ask about the trawler again."

Spinning around, she practically ran to her car. Forget the damn book; she'd get it on the next trip. Home, that's where she needed to be, home in her kitchen with its familiarity, its bits of Shaun surrounding her, like the big island table he'd built and the industrial sink he'd installed.

"It's true, you know," Colin hollered after her.

She continued walking until she reached her car, pressed the key remote, and unlocked the door.

A minute later, she was inside, the groceries on the passenger floor. Her hands strangled the wheel as a shudder ran through her body. In the rearview mirror Colin paced away, arms swinging like posts. The man had the neck of a bulldog.

Sagging forward, Kat set her forehead against the backs of her hands and shuddered out a breath.

No, she thought. Shaun never would have said those things about their life. He was happy. With her and Blake. With the *Kat Lady*. He had loved life to the fullest.

Hadn't he?

Like any normal couple they'd had their arguments. But she had never felt uncertain about their life, never believed he hated operating the trawler. Yes, he'd studied to be a marine biologist, but when his grandfather left him the Victorian and the vessel, Shaun was the first to return to Firewood Island.

"The island's in our blood," he'd told Kat the day they got engaged and talked about going home. *"But what about your degree?"* she'd asked, to which he'd

replied, *"I can teach people more about the sea and its creatures from the deck of a boat than I can as a lab rat."*

Colin Dirks was wrong. Resentful and wrong.

On that thought, she reached to start the ignition. Suddenly her door flung open and a big-shouldered man, silhouetted in the morning sun, blocked her exit. Kat let out a startled gasp.

Chapter Five

"Take it easy." Dane glanced to where the man she'd spoken with disappeared around the corner of the grocery store. He hadn't heard the entire conversation, but from what he'd seen of Kaitlin's body language, he knew the discussion wasn't favorable.

She slumped in the seat. A sigh drifted from her lips. "You really have a knack of showing up at the most unexpected times."

Crouching in the well of the door, Dane pushed back his Indianapolis Colts ballcap, and studied her for a couple seconds. "I didn't like the way he was talking to you."

"Well, that makes two of us."

He wanted to reach in, calm her shaky hands on the wheel. "Who is he?"

"Long story."

"I'm not going anywhere."

Her head turned and their gazes held. Somewhere in the back of his mind it registered that her eyes were the prettiest he'd seen in years. Brown and gold, with specks of green; short, thick lashes the color of a night sky.

She said, "He's my late husband's cousin and he wants to buy my...the *Kat Lady*."

"What do you want to do?" Yes, he'd been meaning to talk to her about restoring the vessel, but this was not how he planned to broach the topic.

She looked toward the trees that edged the rear of the library. Why hadn't he noticed her profile before? The short, straight nose, the tilt to her small chin, the gentle slope of her brow?

"I don't want to sell," she said.

"Then that's your answer."

Again she turned to him, again their gazes locked. "Why do I get the feeling you don't agree?"

"Kaitlin, this is not up to me. It's your property, your decision."

"But you don't agree," she insisted.

He hesitated. He could explain why she should do *something* with the trawler, or he could shrug his shoulders, leave well enough alone. Either way, he sensed a link between them would collapse with her disappointment in him.

Don't be a fool, Dane. You're not that *important to her.* Trouble was, in a dime's worth of days she'd become important to *him.* Just looking at her, dressed in her ankle boots with their pencil-thin heels and those rust-colored slacks, and that green jacket outlining her breasts...

He wanted to kiss her blind. He wanted to lay her down on the seat of her old Civic and—

"What would you do?" she asked in a voice that

dipped his line of vision to her mouth because she'd whispered the question.

He hauled in his libido and hung his head to gain control. If he stood right now, she'd see the evidence of his thoughts.

"Dane?"

Lifting his gaze, he said, "I'd sell the boat." And when her eyes darkened, he added, "Or I'd fix her up and hire someone to put her on the water."

She viewed the trees again. "I don't have the money to fix her." The words were quiet, as if she'd thought them aloud. Turning to him, she smiled. "I have to go. See you tonight?"

He didn't budge. And then, before he could consider the impact, he said, "Only if you let me restore the boat free of charge, but with one condition."

Slowly, her eyes seized his. "What?"

"You let me do whatever I want with the boat."

Her brows bunched. "I don't understand."

"I restore her the way I see fit."

"What do you know about boats?"

"Enough." He rose. "Trust me?"

The interior of the car shadowed her eyes. "Do I have a choice?"

"Always." He moved back and closed her door.

She slid down the window. "Let me think about it." And then she put the vehicle in reverse and backed from the stall. As she drove carefully past where he stood, her eyes clung to his and another jolt of heat zapped through his groin.

Damn it, if you need a woman, Rainhart, go visit some Seattle bar. One-night stands are a dime a dozen there.

He watched her leave the tiny parking lot, enter

Main and head for Shore Road where she turned left and vanished.

Lifting his ballcap, Dane scraped back his hair and blew a long breath. He'd chosen her B and B because of its seclusion. He should've stayed in the east, in the Berkshire Mountains.

But Firewood Island had called to him and he hadn't been able to resist its lure. He hadn't been able to stop yearning for the familiar, for what he knew and understood like the face he saw in the mirror each morning. He hadn't been able to disregard the place of his birth, the hope that he'd find a semblance of peace here.

Instead he'd discovered Kaitlin, a woman from his past. And he wanted her more than he'd ever wanted his ex-wife.

"Dane?" A voice he recognized instantly as his sister's had him turning from where he'd parked the Harley on a side street in the village. "Omigod. It *is* you," she said, hurrying toward him, a rucksack purse banging her hip. Her eyes skimmed the scar along his left jaw, and for a second he saw her hesitate. "When— when did you get back?"

Heart hammering, he waited until she stood in front of him. "Hey, Felicia," he said, purposely using her full name rather than the nickname he'd pronounced at a year-and-a-half. Purposely setting the tone for emotional dissonance.

She raised a blond brow. "What happened to good old Lissa?" She lifted her arms. "And where's my hug? What's it been, three years?"

He stepped forward and set his arms stiffly around his sister, but she'd have none of it and pulled him in close.

"Darn, but it's good to see you." Clasping his cheeks between her hands she rose up and gave him a smacking kiss on the mouth. "I should kick you for not letting us know you were back. When did you get here?"

When he told her he'd been on the island for almost two weeks, her blue eyes widened. The flash of hurt made him cringe. "Why didn't you let us know?"

"I need to be alone for a while." He couldn't explain the logic. Lissa was his sister, the girl he'd shared secrets and dreams with. She was the sister who'd given him tips on talking to girls, who he'd helped more than once sneak out of the house after her midnight curfew. But he still couldn't explain the night sweats and nightmares, the constant, palpable guilt he lived and breathed.

Sunlight filtering through the leafless maples along the street dappled her face as she studied him a moment. "That place changed you." Gently, her fingers touched his jaw where the car's metal had scraped. "Oh, Dane…" Her eyes clouded and her lips pinched together.

This was why he hadn't gone home, why he hadn't called her. Lissa would smother him with pity and heartache. His mother would choke him with her sad looks, and his dad… His dad would quietly stare at him whenever he thought Dane wasn't looking.

You've got things inside you. Kaitlin's words swam across his mind. She'd seen his torment, but she wasn't inclined to fix, to heal the way his family would want to fix and heal.

"Look, I gotta go." He climbed onto the Harley. He had to get out of here before Lissa started crying.

"Wait. What do I tell Mom and Dad? I can't keep this secret, you know."

He drew on his helmet. It had been a mistake to come

into Burnt Bend during the daylight hours. "What they don't know won't hurt them."

Panic flickered across his sister's eyes. "But they're going to find out. The island's too small, and Mom's going to be so hurt. She's been praying for you ever since it happened."

The explosion. Following his divorce, and before the clash between rebels trashed his hands, Dane had incorporated his parents as his in-case-of-emergency contacts. The instant the military notified the senior Rainharts, his mother wanted to fly to Boston while he underwent the surgeries and skin grafts. He'd called his dad and said there would be a No Visitors designation on his hospital records. No doubt that warning hurt, but during those days Dane wanted no one, especially his mother, at his bedside. What was the use of them seeing him burned and scarred and hovering at the periphery of depression?

Yet, while the wounds on his body had mended to a degree, those on his soul still faced a long journey.

No, better to keep them away.

Offering Lissa a half-smile, he said, "Tell them I'm okay, and I'm on the island. At least it's a whole nation closer than Boston."

He cranked the bike to life, flipped down the helmet's visor. With a last nod to his sister, Dane surged the Harley from the curb. He had to get back to that little cabin in the woods, back to Kaitlin—and the difference he felt within her presence. A difference he'd lost in the desert.

At six p.m. sharp, Kat heard a soft knock on the kitchen's back door. She glanced around. Everything stood ready. The table was set with her good china, the vegetables steamed on the stove, a spring salad waited on the counter and she'd taken the chicken from the oven.

She palmed her apron. *Okay, take a breath. It's just Dane. You've known him most of your life.*

As much as she tried to convince herself this was a gratitude dinner because he'd shrugged off her son's indiscretion the other night—and that she was determined to give him a new memory—Kat couldn't stop the dip in her stomach at the thought of seeing the man waiting on the other side of her door.

Come on. He's just a guy. No different than those two you dated last year.

Except, when she'd dated them electricity never shot through her limbs and her legs hadn't gone a little weak.

Lifting her chin, she walked to the door.

Under the deck's light, his eyes were dark as the night behind him.

Oh, God. That incredible smile. Slow, sexy, mesmerizing. No wonder she'd been smitten at thirteen.

He had dressed in black trousers and a slate-blue polo shirt open at the collar where she saw a wedge of dark skin and a dusting of golden hair. The tiny lights strung across the pergola to the left, glinted in his sandy hair. In the two weeks he'd been her guest he'd forgone a visit to the barber. Tonight, his hair appeared to have grown enough to touch the tips of his ears.

"Kaitlin," he said, tugging her gaze back to his.

"Hi." Could she sound any more schoolgirlish? Suddenly she felt underdressed in her stonewashed jeans and rose-colored sweater.

But if he noticed, it had no effect on his deepening

smile as he held out a bottle of wine. As usual, his hands were gloved. Tonight, the leather was butter-soft, the color of his skin and tight as a surgeon's gloves. "Didn't know your favorite," he said, "or if you even had one."

Pleased at his selection, she took the bottle. "Pinot Noir," she murmured, stepping aside to let him into her home. "Actually *this* is my favorite. Thank you."

He followed her into the heart of the kitchen, took a deep sniff. "Mmm. Smells good. I haven't had a home-cooked meal in…. Heck, I can't remember."

At the stove, she slanted a look over her shoulder to where he stood with his hands tucked into his trouser pockets. The irritation from the morning's episode at the library had vanished from his eyes. "You don't cook for yourself?" she asked.

"I do, but it doesn't taste the same."

"The cook never likes his or her own creations."

He chuckled. "I wouldn't call my attempts creations. They're the throw-everything-in-one-pot concoctions."

"Sounds tasty."

"You have no idea," he said drolly.

Grinning, Kat removed the roasting pan from the oven and set it on a metal trivet before lifting the lid to release a chicken-and-sage scented cloud of steam. She extracted a carving knife from a drawer. "Want to do the honors?" she asked, offering the tool.

His gaze went to the knife, then to her face. Carefully, he drew his hands from his trouser pockets. His gloved fingers touched hers in the exchange.

Are the gloves connected to that hurt child? she wanted to ask, but, of course, kept silent. His past was not her business.

"Mom." Blake came into the kitchen. "I'm hungry. When are we eating?"

"In a few minutes," Kat replied. "Have you washed up?"

"Uh-huh." He walked to the worktable where Dane stared down at the roasted chicken. "Hey, Mr. Rainhart. How come you're wearing gloves to cut the meat?"

"Blake," Kat said. "Why don't you put the salad bowls on the table?"

"Okay." His brown eyes, so like hers, gazed at the man, whose face paled under his dark skin. "You okay, Mr. R?"

"I'm fine, Blake. Just trying to figure out where to begin." He shot Kat a crooked smile.

"Oh. Well." Her son pointed to the breast of the chicken. "You're supposed to start with the white meat. That's where my dad used to start, anyway."

"Good choice." Dane set down the knife. "Want to take over? The man of the house should always carve the meat."

Blake's eyes lit. "Sure! I watched my dad lots of times. He could cut meat with his eyes closed."

Actually, Kat thought, amused. *Your daddy was terrible with a carving knife. He shredded the meat like a wood chipper.*

As she prepared the gravy at the stove, she watched Blake pick up the carving knife. For a moment he hesitated. Until now, the only knives she'd allowed him to handle were those beside his plate. His face beamed with excitement.

"Hold it steady," Dane instructed, "and let the blade do the work."

He moved away, just enough to give her son space

and yet be in reach in case he needed help. Kat wondered if Dane realized what was happening, that with every second her son became more enthralled with the man at his elbow.

After Blake sawed off one half of the chicken breast, he set down the knife. "Kinda messy, isn't it?"

"You're doing fine," Dane encouraged.

"No, I'm not." The boy stared at the pile of chunks on the platter. "You finish. I gotta go pee."

"Blake!" Kat gaped at her son. "Way too much information."

"Sorry, I meant I have to go to the washroom." He dashed from the room.

At the worktable, she poured the gravy into its china boat. "Thank you," she said to Dane, "for not turning away from Blake."

Carefully, he laid the knife on the platter before coming around the table to stand close enough that his breath warmed her temple and his scent—something masculine and breezy—filled her lungs. When his knuckle touched her cheek, her body stilled.

Softly he said, "I think about you, Kaitlin."

The words thrilled her, until she realized he hadn't acknowledged her inference about Blake. Suddenly, she wondered if Dane had offered her son a chance to cut meat as a distraction from any personal questions.

She hoped not. She hoped Dane had wanted to teach her son.

Taking up the gravy, she went to the dining table. Distance, even ten feet, allowed her to think, and she needed to think. Trouble was, all through the meal Dane watched Kat with those penetrating eyes. Every glance was a caress on her skin, a kiss on her mouth, a touch to her secret places… Oh, the looks occurred only when Blake was focused on his food and for that she was grateful, but by the time the meal was done, her thoughts were jumbled and her heart a drum in her chest.

Blake helped Dane clear the table and load the dishwasher while she dealt with the leftovers. Ten minutes later, her son disappeared into the living room to watch a sitcom, and Kat became acutely aware that she and Dane were alone.

"Do you have the key to the boatshed?" he asked when she closed the refrigerator on the last container. "I'd like to begin tomorrow."

Of course. He would want to get started ASAP. "Hold on." She hurried to her office, retrieved the key and returned to find him at the back door. Masking her surprise that he'd want to leave so soon—especially after the way he'd whispered *I think about you*—she set the key in his gloved palm. The touch made him flinch. Had she hurt him somehow, pressed too hard on an old wound?

He pocketed the key and the moment was gone. "I had a nice time tonight," he said, voice gruff.

"Me, too." *Let's do it again soon,* she wanted to say.

His gaze settled on her mouth.

Kat stepped back, hugged her waist. No. They couldn't do this again, not when he confused her and tempted her and… It was time for him to go before she did something crazy, like kiss him. She reached for the doorknob. "Good night, Dane."

"See you in the morning."

Still he lingered.

She edged the door closed and, taking the hint along with one last look, he walked across the deck and into the night. Alone again, she turned to face the kitchen.

She could see him still, standing at her worktable, his body pressed close and warm and invading her space.

She could no longer recall how Shaun had looked, standing in the same spot, or how it had felt when *he* invaded her space.

Kat shut her eyes against the guilt of wanting a man in her life again—a man who, she admitted, had trouble relating to her son.

Midnight came and went and still she lay awake. Oh, heck, why pretend sleep was around the corner? Swinging back the quilt, Kat climbed out of bed. She'd always worn an old pair of sweatpants and one of Shaun's ratty flannel shirts during cold winter nights, and in the past four years, that hadn't changed.

In the darkness she felt around the floor with her bare feet, found her slippers, and went downstairs.

Not thirsty or hungry, she bypassed the kitchen and went to her office. For a moment she stood in the doorway, debating. No. She wanted to look at the stars, to breathe in the night air, cool the heat under her skin, the urgency. An urgency she hadn't felt in years.

Dane, of course, was its cause. Dane, who had ridden into her life on a big black bike one rainy afternoon.

Out the back door she went, and over to the edge of the deck where she'd stood recently and he'd told her to *be careful* around him. Her lips twitched. Maybe *he* needed to be careful around *her.*

Hugging her chest, she shivered from the chilled air. Above the serrated tree line, stars glittered like ice chips in a deep, black bowl.

Again she shivered, but not from the cold this time,

from a sense that something moved within the forest to her right.

And, then she saw his tall, dark figure step onto her lawn. He approached slowly. "Couldn't sleep, either?" he asked in a soft, deep voice.

"I thought I heard a raccoon," she said, not wanting to admit what he clearly discerned. "They love digging up my tulips." Which was true; she often sprinkled cayenne pepper around the plants to ward off the creatures.

"And was one here?" He halted in front of her, eyes level with hers, although he stood on the ground and she on the deck.

She felt her heart speed up at his closeness. "If he was, he's gone now. Why aren't you sleeping?"

"Three guesses, Kaitlin." Her breath stalled when he stroked her cheek with a gloved thumb.

"This isn't a good idea," she whispered, unable to tear her gaze from his.

"What isn't?"

"I should…" *Back away.* Except her feet felt as if they'd grown roots.

"What, Kaitlin? What should you do?" The thumb moved across her cheek, and then his fingers gently cupped her chin, tilting her mouth up to meet his.

At the touch of his lips, Kat's first thought was, *He's warm, not cold.* Warm and supple and mobile and— *wow.* He knew how to kiss. He knew what she wanted, what she needed, and, oh yes, what she had been missing for four long years.

Leisurely, he danced his tongue with hers, and she let him. He took her hands, placed them on his shoulders, and she let him. He drew her closer, body to body, and she let him. She gloried in the feel, the sensation of a man's touch. Of Dane's touch.

Her skin tingled, her pulse leapt. Every molecule vibrated and still she couldn't get enough. Someone groaned. Her? Him? She was past caring. Her body had liquefied, readying itself for—

He eased her away. "Kaitlin." His voice was thick, rough. "We need to stop."

Blinking, she stared up into a face shadowed in night. His blue eyes were more serious than she'd ever seen them. That seriousness had her stepping back, almost stumbling.

What had she done? What had possessed her to kiss a man, a virtual stranger, as though she were some wanton woman?

She'd loved Shaun.

She missed Shaun.

He had been her hero for all their married years.

How could she feel passion for another man? Shaun had been her soul mate. At thirteen, her adoration of Dane had been the result of pubescent hormones, and now she was allowing a whole new set of hormones to dictate her actions. She'd been too lonely, was all.

"I'm sorry," she said, and wiped her wrist across her mouth as if to eliminate his taste. But of course the gesture erased nothing. That masculine mouth, so ardent and tender, had done its job. She would remember him long into the night, long into tomorrow. And far beyond.

His eyes narrowed, and she nearly chuckled. Did he think he repulsed her? Oh, but he was wrong because, heaven help her, she would give anything for him to step forward and kiss her again. And again.

"You may be sorry," he said, voice flat. "But *I'm* not. You're a sexy woman. Any man would give his right arm to have you in his bed. Have a good night, Kaitlin." Pivoting, he turned to stride up the stone pathway to the cabin.

Kat watched him go. *You don't understand,* she wanted to call out. She hadn't meant the apology in *that* way. She was confused, didn't he know? Eight years of marriage filled her past, her memories—not to mention a love that had produced a son.

Talking to Dane, standing close enough to feel his body's heat, smelling the soap he used, kissing him under the night sky…. All smudged bits and pieces of that marriage, of Shaun. Soon, her husband would be no more. Even now, as she stood in the frosty night with an owl hunting its quarry, she could not recall the details of his face. That he had blue eyes and curly brown hair and emitted a laugh big as the ocean, she remembered easily. But minutiae like the bow of his lips, the creases near his eyes, the contour of his left thumb, or the outline of his Adam's apple, those she could no longer recall without the support of a photograph.

"You'd be wise to stay away from me." Kat sighed at Dane's earlier words. She hadn't heeded him. She'd moved forward, straight into his arms.

But the guilt of that step was nothing compared to the guilt of hungering for more of the same. And thinking, *After twenty-two years, I've finally kissed him.*

Before she ran up the path and barged into his cabin, she spun around and ran to her own door. But no matter how fast she hurried through the kitchen, and up the stairs to her bedroom, no matter how quickly she crawled back under the covers, she could not escape the thrill of kissing Dane Rainhart. *At last.*

On the second floor, Blake carefully closed the wooden slat of the blinds on his bedroom window. When he'd heard voices in the backyard, he had taken a peek, only to see his mom and Mr. Rainhart in a lip lock.

Confused, he got back in bed. Okay, he thought Mr. Rainhart was pretty cool tonight at dinner and when he'd worked on the Harley this morning…

That was different!

His mom kissing the guy changed things. Sure, Blake knew Mom might want to see another man one day, but he thought it'd be way in the future. Like when Blake went to college or something.

He swallowed hard. What if the guy started taking Mom out to restaurants, or over to the mainland? What if he started hanging around the house instead of staying in his cabin?

Once Blake'd heard his Grams tell Mom that "life was passing her by" and that she was in the "prime of her life."

But did she have to kiss Mr. Rainhart? And then Blake remembered…The guy often carried a knife and sometimes his eyes could look right through you.

He didn't tonight. Tonight, he'd been real nice. He'd even called Blake "the man of the house" when he gave him the carving knife. And, wow, he'd felt ten feet tall right there.

Blake reached to turn on his bedside lamp. He stared at the photo beside it. In the picture, he was seven. His dad had one hand on Blake's shoulder while they stood on the bow of the *Kat Lady* moored to the pier down by the boatshed. Mom had taken the picture three months before his dad drowned.

Sometimes, Blake's chest felt funny when he looked at the picture. Before that awful day, his mom had laughed a lot. Now all she did was worry.

She never said anything, especially to his aunties and Gram, but he knew. Knew she hated when the cottages sometimes stayed empty for days in the winter. Not that they were poor, but things weren't the same as they'd been when his dad was alive and ran his fishing business.

Sometimes Blake wished Mom would sell the boat. Sometimes, he couldn't bear thinking of it gone.

Suddenly, his heart thumped hard. Was Mr. Rainhart thinking of buying the *Kat Lady?* Was that why he'd kissed Mom? So he could get on her good side and start hanging with her and then move in?

That's what happened to Blake's best friend. One minute, Gerry and his mom were living fine by themselves, the next minute she got married and his stepdad started ordering Gerry around.

Blake curled into a ball. Tomorrow he'd talk to Gerry, see what his pal would've done differently to stop what happened to him.

For the first time since his father died, he slept with the light on.

Chapter Six

Dawn outlined the treetops in an ashy pink when Dane inserted the key to unlock the boatshed doors. He'd had a restless night, at best sleeping four hours after walking the shoreline shortly before midnight. The dreams hadn't kept him awake. No, this time it'd been Kaitlin.

Last night he'd kissed her, then gone to bed thinking about her arms around his neck, thinking about the way her small body fit his so damned perfectly, and reliving the sweet taste of her mouth, and how her dark hair gleamed in the starlight.

Oh, he'd known what he was doing when he stood in her kitchen and said, *"I think about you, Kaitlin."*

Hell. What kind of game was he trying to play?

That was the joke of it. He hadn't been playing at all. He'd been dead serious. She was beginning to make him feel in a way he hadn't in years. Around her, he'd begun to yearn for something bright and positive, something that made him forget the darkness, the sadness. And he suspected that Kaitlin, more than anything or anyone before, would offer him that bright, positive speck.

Stupid damn fool, he thought. *Until—unless—you sort out your crap and get your head on straight, she's off-limits.*

He pushed the broad boatshed doors wide, letting in the early light. Musty scents of dust, old wood and stale salty air struck Dane's nose. Above his head, the *Kat Lady*'s prow rose high and dignified while the lines of her hull curved seaward—as though she smelled freedom beyond the yawning entrance.

Dane studied the trawler. She wasn't new; he assumed an easy thirty-five years by her make and design. She'd been worked hard, likely as a lobster trawler on the Atlantic coast, before someone transported her west to fish in the Pacific off Firewood Island.

A decade or more ago, a coat of white or yellow paint might have been applied to her wood, although he couldn't determine the exact hue with the barnacle growth that had collected during idle times, and the torment high tides and whitecaps affected.

Someone had jacked a thirty-foot aluminum construction ladder against the boat's hull, so he climbed aboard into the cockpit—the deck behind the pilothouse.

Here things weren't in any better shape. The hardwood was scuffed almost white and desperately needed an oiling, and the anchor had a clump of dried seaweed attached to one hook.

Dane opened the wooden door to the pilothouse, stepped into the galley and recognized Kaitlin's reluctance to part with the vessel. Here were touches of the man she'd married: his sailor's cap and yellow slicker on a hook behind the door, and a trio of pictures of the family on the wall opposite the helm and captain's chair. Two photos were of Kaitlin, Blake and his father on the boat, and one had them sitting on the deck behind the Victorian, surrounded by potted flowers.

Dane moved closer to study the photographs. Her husband had been a robust, barrel-chested man, with dark hair and the ear-to-ear grin he recognized from last night when Kaitlin's boy went on and on about how his dad "was the best sailor ever." Likely the kid was making a point for Dane's sake, except he had been more interested in watching Kaitlin at the time. Sitting at the head of the table, she'd looked at her son with such a sad smile that Dane had had to glance away.

Remembering, he turned from the pictures on the wall. She still loved her husband. Which, he hated to admit, was better for him. Her unresolved emotions would help put a stop to his fantasies.

He scanned the remainder of the helm—and noticed the blue jacket tossed on the bench beside the captain's chair. The corner of a book peeked from under the garment.

Dane pushed the jacket aside.

Not a novel, an album.

His heart thumped hard. He knew what he'd find among the pages. Photos. Dozens of photos of Kaitlin's dead husband. Family photos. Had Kaitlin brought the album here to thumb through the pictures, and remember days and events and happier times?

"Have you even opened the doors of the shed since Shaun died?"

Oh, yeah, he'd heard most of the conversation at the

library; the jackass confronting Kaitlin had the voice of a foghorn.

Tamping back his anger, he studied the jacket. Not Kaitlin's—her son's. Dane pictured the boy sitting in the captain's chair, poring over the album, remembering moments with his father the way Dane recalled his own youth on Firewood Island when his grandfather took him fishing during summer vacations. On the old man's trawler, Dane had learned to love the sea.

Hell, if he was honest with himself, he'd admit there was more to this restoration job than the *Kat Lady;* he hoped to restore those summer memories—and set Iraq into a far distance.

He hadn't considered the ghost of the man who once owned the vessel, or the boy's memories. He hadn't considered Kaitlin's abiding love for her late husband. Nor had he considered how he'd feel about all three situations.

Pursued by a horde of ghosts, Dane climbed from the pilothouse. He needed to ride his Harley, feel the slap of wind on his face, the thrum of the engine vibrating through his body. He needed to clear his mind, the ache in his chest and knew that no matter how far and fast he rode, he would return just as mixed up as when he'd left.

He went anyway.

Kat picked up the tray balancing three lattes and walked to the table in the front corner of Coffee Sense, the quaint little shop where she and her sisters often cooled down after their Saturday walks. Together, Kat, Lee and Addie walked or jogged the island's shoreline trail thrice weekly, a habit they formed four years ago as a result of the stress and chaos in Kat's and Addie's lives back then. When Lee returned to the island after the infidelity of her first husband, the exercise routine had become a means of reaffirming the bonds of love and friendship among sisters.

This Saturday morning the walk had eased some of the tension riding Kat's shoulders the last four days. On Tuesday, she'd had to pay Zeb Jantz, the local handyman, to repair a leaking drainage pipe in the laundry room, as well as install a new washer when the old one died—all on the same day. Zeb had been wonderful about the cost; he'd only charged her for the parts even though the old man worked in her laundry room for three hours, tearing out and replacing a section of ancient pipe.

And then there was the call from Blake's fifth-grade teacher Wednesday afternoon. Apparently, he'd been caught cheating during a routine math test, a test Kat knew her son should have aced with his eyes closed. Math was his favorite subject. Since first grade, he had never received a mark below ninety.

Topping it all off was her obsession with Dane. She hadn't seen him since their kiss more than a week ago. She knew he worked in the boatshed, because she'd walked down the weedy, wooded trail to its delta where the shed, tackle shack and graveled parking area were located. With the exception of the motorcycle waiting in the shadow of the shed, the place had looked as deserted as she felt.

Kat had been unable to go farther. Above the sound of the lapping waves, and the wind soughing in the trees, she heard the hum of a power tool, possibly a sander—and the raucousness of heavy metal music. The noise startled her on two levels. First, she never would have guessed Dane to like such music and, second, Colin was right. Since the boat was dry-docked, she had avoided the shed. Looking, listening, she'd wondered why. Why had she kept the doors locked four years?

Because I wasn't ready.

And now? Are you ready now?

She set the latte tray in the center of the bistro table where the windows offered a view of the boardwalk and cove. A hundred yards to the left, Lee's red-and-white floatplane rocked gently on the water, waiting for two passengers and pilot Peyton Sawyer to board.

Lee had given up flying last October when she'd given birth to her daughter Olivia. Now she ran the business from her office upstairs, directly across the landing from the office of her lawyer husband, Rogan Matteo. Both Kat and Addie had cheered when their eldest sister finally admitted Rogan was The One. After the ugliness she had gone through with her ex, Lee had deserved a fine man in her corner, and Rogan certainly fit the bill.

Just as Skip Dalton fit into Addie's corner after the hell *she* had gone through having to give up their first child.

Thank God for guys with heart, Kat thought. Which brought her straight back to Dane. She suspected that beneath that gruff veneer there beat a kind and generous heart. And that's what scared her.

"Hey." Lee tapped Kat's forearm. "Earth calling Kat, come in, please."

She blinked, refocused. "Sorry. I had something on my mind."

"You don't say," Addie drawled. "So dish."

Kat sighed. "I had to buy a new washing machine this week." She explained what happened, avoiding her worries about the expenditure.

"Oh, hon," Lee said, reading Kat clearly. "Why didn't you say? How much do you need?"

"Lee and I can split the amount," Addie put in. "You can pay us back whenever you can."

Kat shook her head. "Thanks, but I'm okay for now." She'd have to cut a few corners, but she would manage. Somehow.

"Your renter hasn't left, has he?" Addie asked.

"No." She picked up her napkin, tore off a corner.

Lee narrowed her green eyes. "What's going on, Kat? Is he still acting strange?"

"What?" This from Addie. "You've got a man staying at your place who's—"

"Who's nothing." Kat glared at Lee. "He's not strange, just…different."

"Jeez, Kat." Addie again. "You need to tell us these things."

"Why? He's fine."

"Why? Because you live out of town. Because you live down a country road, *away* from everyone else. It was fine when Shaun was alive, but now…"

Kat held up her palm. "Okay, I appreciate your concerns, but, honestly, Dane is a decent person."

Sipping her latte, Lee lifted an auburn brow. "Just so you know," she said, "I met his sister a few days ago in Dalton Foods. Apparently, he wants nothing to do with his parents."

"His sister shouldn't be gossiping," Kat snapped.

"It wasn't gossip, sis," Lee said gently. "Felicia is very worried about her brother. Her comment came from exasperation and concern. He won't let her or any of his family near him and won't even tell them he's staying at your B and B. She's worried he's suffering from PTSD and not getting the help he requires."

"Good grief." Kat sat back, amazed. "For someone

you barely know, she certainly told you a lot of personal stuff."

Lee frowned. "She's belongs to a book club I joined last summer. One day we went for coffee, discovered a bunch of similar interests and…" she shrugged "…a friendship evolved."

Before Kat could think it through, she said, "Well, just so *you* know, Dane and I are friends."

Intrigued, Addie leaned forward. "How friendly?"

"Enough that I'm letting him fix the *Kat Lady*."

Her sisters' mouths fell open. "You are?" they said in unison.

Kat looked out the window. Once, the trawler, which had been in the O'Brien family for over thirty years, had plowed through the cove's waters to fish far offshore under the guidance of Shaun's grandfather. Some days Kat missed the old guy as much as his grandson.

"Are you planning to sell the boat?" Addie wanted to know.

Kat looked down at her mug. "I'm not sure. Colin Dirks wants it."

"The weasel?" Lee asked. She hadn't liked the man any more than Kat.

"The same," she confirmed.

For several moments they looked out at the sunny day, the dazzling waters.

"Keep the boat," Addie said at last. "Don't let it go, Kat. Once Dane restores it, find someone who'll run it for you."

The way Shaun had. Kat couldn't wrap her mind around the image. Until she pictured Dane—feet planted, broad shoulders squared—standing at the helm. Dane, who apparently knew all about boats.

Kat looked at Lee. "Did Felicia say anything about Dane's years in the service?"

For the first time, her older sister hesitated. "Only that he was with Oliver when he died."

Oliver Duvall, the father of Lee's little girl, the man she might have married if he hadn't been ambushed. No wonder Lee had hooked up with Dane's sibling; they had more in common than books.

Lee went on, "Both Felicia and Rogan want me to talk to Dane for Olivia's sake and someday I will. But Rogan is Olivia's father in every way that counts." Her eyes filled with deep emotion. "He loves her to pieces. God," she said, shaking her head. "I can't believe how lucky I am."

"You're crazy about him," Kat observed.

"Oh, yeah. Totally."

Kat glanced at Addie, who wore a dreamy smile of her own.

Probably thinking of Skip and their family, Kat mused before a sting pierced her chest. Once, she'd lived what her sisters now lived. Then Shaun had gone fishing on his cousin's trawler even though the weather forecasted a storm.

She had begged him not to go. Suddenly, the nip of resentment she kept tamped down all these years punched hard.

Damn him. He knew better.

Dane wouldn't have gone.

The instant the thought registered, she sat back in her chair. How she knew he wouldn't have left her and Blake, she wasn't sure. She only knew his choice would've been different than her husband's.

What had Colin Dirks said when he chased her into

the library parking lot? *"Shaun wished you wouldn't have forced him back to the island. He hated it here."*

"Kat." Addie leaned forward. "What is it?"

"I have to go," she said, rising from her chair. "Tell Blake I'll pick him up in a half hour," she told her youngest sister.

"He can stay the afternoon if he wants," Addie said. "Danny's staying."

Danny was Lee's eight-year-old stepson. When Kat and her sisters went for their Saturday power walks, they left all the children with Skip or Rogan. Today was Skip's turn. "Fine," Kat said. "I'll be at your place at four." And then she rushed out the door, hurrying to her car.

She had to see the boat, had to see what was on its deck, in the pilothouse, the galley—

Proof, she needed proof Colin was wrong.

She had no idea what she would find on the vessel. That it might be something she didn't want to know scared her clean to the bone. Seeing Dane again, however, chilled her soul. How could she ask a man obviously hiding from his family, *Would you go against your family's wishes?*

Dane heard the sound of an engine on the trail leading down to the boatshed. His heart rate accelerated. *Kaitlin?*

From the hip pocket of his coveralls, he drew his gloves and tugged them on, and waited until the motor died and the vehicle's door slammed.

Seated on the overturned bucket outside the shed doors, he continued to clean the engine's water strainer. Beyond the slip of beach, a two-foot chop deposited froth on the shore. With the salt-tinged wind came the scent of rain and in the westerly sky a low navy bank of clouds hovered. A storm was on its way.

"Hi."

His heart kicked at the sound of her voice. He turned his head toward the corner of the building.

Had she come back from one of those sisterly walks she'd mentioned that night at her dinner table? Or was she en route to join them? And what the hell did it matter? She was here, wasn't she? Outlined in yellow and white spandex, worn Nikes and red headband.

"Hey."

The afternoon's pale light placed a hint of deep copper among the dark strands of her hair as she approached the yawing doorway. Dane rose slowly, saw surprise flicker across her brown eyes as she looked inside.

"You've already sanded the whole hull in…a week?" she asked.

He shrugged. With the dreams claiming most of his nights, the boat had been a 24/7 godsend.

She shook her head. "Last I remember, the hull was in terrible shape. I thought it would take a month or…more."

Usually scraping and sanding took longer. Rather than explaining, he said, "I don't have anything else to do."

She walked inside. Trailing in her wake, he smelled her skin, heated from her exercise, and between his legs his blood quickened.

His gaze took in the curve of her shoulders, the way the breathable long-sleeved T-shirt shaped her waist. He liked how the spandex clung to the flare of her hips.

She was an outdoorsy kind of woman, working in her garden, walking and running trails. What his ex-wife obtained at gyms and tanning salons, Kaitlin achieved naturally.

"I'm going up to the pilothouse," she said, nodding at the ladder.

"I haven't started on board yet."

His visitor studied him a second. "I'm not checking up on you, Dane. I'm looking for something."

He moved toward her. "What is it? Maybe I can help."

"I don't know." She glanced to the top rung. "Actually, it has to do with my late husband."

"Something he left behind?"

She frowned. "In a way." Then she climbed the ladder and for about five seconds he got a great view of her small round butt and those strong runner's legs before she disappeared over the edge of the boat and ducked down into the cabin.

Dane debated. Should he join her in the galley, help her search, or go back to work on the engine's strainer? *Hell.* What he really wanted was to smell her some more.

Grabbing hold of the ladder, he scrambled up and hopped onto the deck. As he entered the pilothouse, she half-turned toward him, album in her hands. "I've wondered where this was. Blake must have brought it here one time when his dad…" She hugged the book to her chest. "I'm glad it was here. I'd worried that it might be lost."

Her gaze roved the confined area. The light beyond the narrow, horizontal windows enveloped the room in dusk and painted the line of her throat with shadows, the line that dipped into a hollow made for kisses. Somewhere in the succeeding silence, he became aware that she had focused on him—and what held his attention.

His gaze lifted to hers. A sigh crossed her lips.

God help him.

Before he hauled her to him and devoured that mouth, devoured *her,* he strode to the opposite side of the captain's chair. "So," he said, intent on the windshield and the ocean beyond, and hiding the swell at his groin. "You found what you were searching for." Now that she'd retrieved the album he wanted her gone.

"No." Pause. "I'd come to find out if my husband hated living with me."

Soft and full of resignation, the statement angled him around. "Hated living with you?"

She blew a long whispery breath. "His cousin, the one he went fishing with that…that last time, said Shaun told him so."

The man at the library parking lot? "Is this cousin a reliable source?"

"They grew up together. He was like a brother to Shaun."

Dane wanted to smack the cousin. First for uttering such insensitive words to Kaitlin and, second, for voicing a statement that could never be refuted by a dead man.

"Don't believe it, Kaitlin."

Her eyes hung on his. "No? Then why did he let the boat get into such terrible shape? Why didn't he take better care of her? Look at that mildew damage on that wall over there." She pointed to where the man's slicker hung behind the door. "And the salt grime on the windshield and all these scratches and chips…" Her gaze dropped to the scuffed hardwood. "I never noticed any of this before. I was just so happy with my life." She looked at Dane and his heart rolled over. To keep from rushing to the other side of the chair, he fisted his hands, rooted his feet.

She said, "I thought Shaun was happy, too. But now…" Again, she scanned the interior. "Now, I wonder."

"He was happy," Dane said. "A man doesn't have a photo of his wife and kid on the wall beside him if he's not happy."

Over her shoulder, she cast a look at the picture he indicated. "Maybe that was for show, to keep Blake and I from suspecting his true feelings." She returned her gaze to Dane. "Want to know something? When I drove here from the village, the thing that scared me most was seeing you again. It's been eight days since you came to dinner."

He quirked a smile. "Only eight, huh?"

Her gaze fell to the window again. "I loved my husband, Dane."

"I know you did."

"I'd give anything to have him back with us."

He nodded. Waited.

She said, "I don't know if he hated living on the island. I don't know if he hated living with me. We seldom argued. We went on dates." She looked away, her face flushed. "The sex was good. And often." He watched her swallow. "I miss that," she whispered. Her face turned to him. "Is it bad to want someone else as much as you once wanted your spouse? Maybe even more?"

Argh. If she didn't stop, didn't get out of here, he'd have her on this chair. Or the floor. Or the bench by the wall.

"Kaitlin, I'm not a man you want to hook up with for…" *Sex.* He sighed. "There's stuff you don't know about me—"

She did what he could not do himself. She circled the chair, wrapped her arms around his neck and kissed him.

Dane could do only one thing. He let himself fall into the essence that was Kaitlin.

Chapter Seven

Oh! Kat thought as Dane hoisted her to his waist, and she bent over his head, kissing, kissing, kissing. *Oh-oh-oh!* He felt so good. Beyond good. Wonderful. Exceptional. *Glorious.*

In a spiral dance, he set her against the wooden instrument panel. A moan escaped her throat when he tugged the spandex from her waist, and his gloved fingers skimmed her hips, settling her into position.

She heard the *zing* of his zipper, felt him hot and hard against her flesh. *"Yes."* Closing her eyes, she bowed toward him, urgent now, needy and wanton. "Please, Dane."

"Kaitlin."

And then he was in her, deep in her, and they thrashed together quick, hard—faster, faster, *faster.* Sweat popped from her forehead, slicked against the heat and strength of his neck. His hands gripped her jerking hips; her arms clutched his damp, muscled back. *Please... now...yes—*

His body tightened, shuddered and she shuddered with him.

Against her throat he groaned long and deep, and the sound held her in thrall, brought a secret smile to her lips. Tenderly, she kissed his jaw where the scar rippled under her mouth.

"Kaitlin," he said hoarsely; she opened her eyes.

Ten feet away a photo hung on the wall—her husband and Blake flanking Kat—and suddenly Shaun's eyes seemed not to laugh, but instead glimmered in sadness.

What had she done? And right here, in this pilot-house, in Shaun's home away from home. Except Shaun was dead. *Dead, Kat. It's been four years, and you need to move on. So stop feeling guilty.*

But she did. God knew why, but shame drifted like a subtle wind through her veins.

Pushing against Dane's chest, she said, "I need to go pick up my son at my sister's house." An excuse, she knew, because it was just after lunch, but her remark had him stepping away, adjusting his clothes, while she hopped down and adjusted hers.

"Bye," she murmured, hurrying across to the stairs.

"Kaitlin, wait."

She hesitated, hand gripping the banister. She refused to turn, to look at him for fear she would fling into his arms again.

He stopped behind her left shoulder and for several heartbeats said nothing, though she felt the warmth of his breath against her ear.

"Thank you," he said softly.

Gratitude, as though she'd done him a favor. Kat wanted to cry. She wanted him to tell her what they did was right and perfect and that it might be the start of something beautiful between them.

"Sure." Heart hurting, she scrambled up the stairs.

Outside, she ran to the Honda. Behind the wheel again, she backed all the way up the forested trail until she reached the circular drive in front of her home.

In the carport, she disregarded the big Harley waiting for its rider. The moment she saw him in the rain on the machine, she should have known her life wouldn't be the same.

Finally in her kitchen, her familiar, warm kitchen, she sat at the worktable and put her face into her hands. She'd had mindless, ten-minute sex with a virtual stranger. Okay, not quite a stranger, but seeing someone after two decades didn't make them your best friend.

And, be honest, Kat. The sex had been far from mindless.

Truth was, Dane saturated her mind and heart during those frantic, short moments. Heck, at this very moment, her every hormone, nerve ending and fiber felt possessed by him.

She lifted her head, stared across the room and the windows framing the overcast day.

They hadn't used protection.

They'd just…gone at it.

What if—this second—they were making a baby? On her private calendar, the time was right.

Oh, Kat. You silly, foolish woman. How could you be so dumb! You can not afford a child at this time of your life. And Dane… Where on earth would he fit into the picture—if he even wanted to fit?

The more she thought, the more agitated she became, until she rose and paced her kitchen.

What would Blake think?

And her sisters? Both had gotten pregnant by men who weren't there for the births of their children. And now here she was, possibly in the same condition. Three sisters, three unexpected pregnancies. Never mind her mother, who had kept the identity of Kat's father a secret all her life… What a family!

Stop it. You're overreacting about something that might not be happening. The thought had Kat pressing a protective palm to her stomach. A pregnancy would cause a lot of upheaval yet, oddly, imagining no life stung her eyes.

At the front door, someone knocked. She wasn't expecting a renter today, so it had to be one of her sisters—not a surprise after the way she'd left them this morning.

It was Dane. With worried blue eyes. "Good," he said. "You haven't left yet."

She'd told him she needed to pick up Blake. That didn't mean she couldn't have a moment to herself to assemble what had just occurred in her husband's boat. "I'm leaving shortly." She would go uptown, get some groceries for tonight, walk the boardwalk—anything to get away from the house—before it was time to get Blake.

Dane remained motionless. "I only need a minute. Can I come in?"

She stepped aside and he entered, extracting the air from her space.

"Are you all right?" he asked when she'd closed the door.

"Fine." She headed back to her kitchen. "And by the way, you're welcome."

"Kaitlin—ah, hell. You have no idea how sorry I am for…. Hell." Sighing, he trailed her into the room redolent with baking and spices. "These past couple years, I've been…different. Sometimes I say things—" Another sigh. "I regret them afterward."

Behind the worktable, she faced him. Her heart hammered between her ribs. He hadn't worried about a possible baby. His only concern had been how she viewed him, that in her eyes he was still the good guy.

Kat stared at the man across the room. How could she have missed the arrogance, the self-centered—

He said, "Are you on birth control?"

She forced her hands to remain at her sides, not to defend her middle. He would put it on her. "I've been widowed four years." Which sounded as though life passed her by, so she added, "And the men I dated weren't what I expected." Which gave away too much about how she felt about this man, and what they had done in the boathouse.

His eyes didn't waver.

Raising her chin, she clarified, "I never had a reason for birth control. Until today. And then everything went so…so fast." *Because I went a little crazy for you.*

Swallowing, he flicked a look at her stomach. "I want you to know—" His eyes rose, seized hers. "Kaitlin, if you're pregnant because of today, I won't disappear or shirk my responsibilities if you choose to keep the baby. I won't be a deadbeat dad."

So. He *had* considered the risk. She nearly sagged with relief, and took back her disgruntled thoughts. And he hadn't said *it,* but *the baby.* "Thank you."

"How long before your next period?"

"Ten days."

He clipped a nod. "You'll tell me one way or the other?"

"I'll tell you if I'm late."

His shoulders drooped slightly as he caught the back of the stool in front of him. Again his gaze surveyed her stomach. "I wouldn't be unhappy," he said quietly, then straightened, and walked past her, out the mudroom door.

Kat dropped onto her stool. "I wouldn't be unhappy either," she murmured when the door clicked closed. "If it was just me to consider."

But she had a son. Who would never understand her relationship, such as it was, with Dane or why she hadn't been more careful. How could he when she barely understood it herself?

Dane stood at the window of the cabin's eating nook, staring out at the soft rainfall dampening the woods. The day had grayed, bringing with it a mist that rolled off the Pacific and enveloped the environment. Everywhere water dripped from the barren trees and ferny undergrowth.

Amazing how quick the weather changed on the island. Within minutes of Kaitlin leaving the boathouse, the rain descended.

He scraped at his damp hair. What had he been thinking to take her like that? Without consideration for her protection, or a stroke of tenderness or a soft word.

Yeah, she'd been as hot for him as he had for her, but that was no excuse. He should've been man enough to control himself, to be a gentleman, not a sex-starved beast.

Dammit. Rotating around, he scrutinized the cabin he kept to military precision, a precision he hated. Why hadn't he been that precise, that *in control* with Kaitlin?

Because with her you were free for the first time in years, maybe in your life.

He had to get out of here, take the bike and ride. Striding across the room, he grabbed his keys off the kitchen counter.

Outside, the mist altered to a hard drizzle that came straight down and pelted the earth, creating pools in the smallest hollow. When he walked into the carport he saw that it stood empty except for his Harley; she'd gone, escaping, no doubt, the way he wanted to escape. The thought sent a shaft of remorse through Dane. She didn't deserve to have her life screwed up by him. She'd been fine before he came along, before he kissed her, before he took what he had wanted since that first day when he turned his head and hooked onto her brown eyes under that orange umbrella.

God help him if she was pregnant. He wasn't father material. Phoebe, his ex, had wanted a family almost immediately after their wedding, but he'd kept putting her off with all sorts of reasons—they needed to build their financial base, he hadn't finished his overseas tour, he wanted her to go with him to the Congo and join a medical group to help the impoverished.

Phoebe was an excellent nurse, had been for ten years, but with their marriage her goals changed. *"My ovaries aren't getting any younger,"* she'd told him.

After five years, she'd gotten tired of waiting, tired of his excuses. No surprise when his CO handed over the divorce papers—couriered by cargo plane into the desert three summers ago—while Dane performed surgery on an Iraqi child caught by an EFP—explosively formed penetrator.

He'd been so full of himself. Full of medical intelligence, expertise and techniques. Full of arrogance and ego, and believing as head trauma surgeon he alone could make a difference in a country ravaged by war and dissention.

His arrogance had steered him away from Phoebe, away from his family.

Grimly, Dane secured his rain gear and helmet, straddled the bike. *Damn it.* Where had that self-serving attitude gotten him? Back to the island of his birth. And into the arms of a woman he'd forgotten existed until three weeks ago, a woman who could be carrying his child this instant.

He kicked the bike awake. The wet, forested trail beckoned. He took it at full throttle.

Tuesday after school Blake ran down the path to the boathouse. Almost two months had passed since he'd gone through the photo album. Sometimes, he forgot about the boat—and his dad. When was the last time he even looked at his dad's picture on the night table in his bedroom?

The night Mom kissed Dane.

Mom. Jeez, what was going on with her lately? Every time he turned around she was at him about something. Like the second he hit the door five minutes ago, she'd bitten his head off about not taking his inhaler to school again this morning.

Didn't she get that it wasn't cool to puff on an inhaler in front of everybody? Man, how many times had he told her he was okay, that he didn't participate that hard in gym class? He didn't need Ms. Coglin holding on to his inhaler every time the class went through a bunch of stupid basketball drills.

It all started two weeks ago when Troy Challis saw

Blake take a puff in the shower room before warm-up and called him puny. Some of the other guys had laughed along with dorkhead Troy and now they all called him that stupid name every time the teachers weren't around.

Blake broke into a sprint; his asthmatic lungs screamed for air. He *hated* having asthma. He hated the way his mom always hovered over him about the dumb condition.

He wished his dad was alive so he could ask him what to do about Troy. And that was another thing, how could he *forget* to look at his dad's picture? How could he be forgetting his dad?

On a throaty gasp, he stopped, bent and grabbed his knees. His jaw hung slack and saliva dribbled from his lips as he hauled air into his mouth. His heart banged his ribs like a baseball. If he wasn't careful, he'd have an attack right in the middle of the path and no one would know.

Those guys might call him puny, but he didn't want to die like a fish, flopping around on the ground.

Slowly, his breathing quieted and he walked the rest of the way to the boatshed. His mom thought he was in his bedroom finishing his homework, but he'd sneaked out through the front door while she was in the kitchen, baking a batch of muffins.

At the boathouse door, he quickly inserted the key, then stepped into the dusky interior. Already his eyes and nose registered a difference, something not quite…right. On the left wall he slapped the light switch. His mouth dropped open.

The *Kat Lady* lay as always in her cradle, except she wasn't the *Kat Lady*. This boat had her hull's exterior scrubbed and sanded down to the grain of the wood.

What was going on? Had his mom hired someone and not told him? And why hadn't she told him? Was she going to sell the boat?

Blake ran to the ladder, scrambled up to the deck. Okay, okay. Everything looked the same here…everything except for the big, hand-held sander sitting on the floor.

He flew up into the pilothouse, his eyes searching wildly. His blue jacket hung on the back of the chair. For a moment he breathed a relieving sigh. And then realized he never would've hung the coat on the chair. For the past year he made a point of tossing his clothes around his room because he wanted to be like a normal guy, one without asthma, guys who didn't hang up their clothes like some prissy girl. Gerry's room was a cool mess.

Blake stared at the jacket. Somebody had hung it up. His mom? No, his mom would've taken the coat back to the house and asked him why it was on the *Kat Lady*. The guy fixing the boat?

A slow burn rose in Blake's cheeks. How dare he touch his coat. And his album! Somebody had looked through his album. He never left it lying open like that on the seat of the chair.

He felt like one of the three bears in *Goldilocks. Who's been eating my porridge? Sitting in my chair? Sleeping in my bed?*

Snatching up jacket and album, Blake surveyed the galley. He had to hide the album. The fact that somebody had gawked at the pictures felt worse than Troy-the-tool's stupid name calling.

But where would the book be safe from whoever was changing his dad's boat? 'Cause already the *Kat Lady* was different. The lichens and barnacles and mildew collected when his dad lived were history, which was like another little piece of his dad vanishing along with the memories in Blake's head, the ones he needed photos to remember.

Wrapping his jacket around the book, he decided to hide it off the boat where nobody could look at the photos again, where not even his mom would find them—or find out he'd snuck into the boatshed in the first place.

Climbing from the vessel, Blake felt a little better. For darned sure, no one was ever going to take this part of his dad away.

"You okay, honey?" Kat's younger sister Addie asked over the phone Wednesday, an hour after Kat arrived home from their walk. "You were awfully quiet today."

Because I might be carrying Dane's child, she wanted to say. *And if I am, how do I tell Blake?*

Her son seemed out of sorts these days, holing up in his room and muttering single syllable responses when she asked a question or tried to start a conversation. Suspicion had her wondering if it had something to do with Dane…or the album in the boat. Which she'd forgotten to retrieve after she ran from Dane.

She rubbed her forehead. What was she to do about the man renting her cabin?

She hadn't seen him since he appeared on her doorstep minutes after they made love—correction, did the ten-minute bump-and-grind—and he'd wanted notification the moment she knew whether or not his swimmers had landed ashore.

Pure and simple, her life was a mess of Gordian knots she had no idea how to untangle.

Phone pressed between shoulder and ear, Kat again

tallied the right-hand column in her ledger. Yep, expenses for March had gained on profits. Question was, could she hang on until the *Kat Lady* was restored? Or should she contact Colin, tell him the boat was for sale and ask for an advance payment?

Kat's heart pounded at the concept of losing the vessel to *that* man. There had to be another solution, there just had to be.

"Kat?" Addie's voice drifted into her ear.

"Hang on. Almost finished with these figures…" A hundred-eighty-three for groceries last week, against a five-hundred-sixty-five washer. Profit margin nil, liability three-eighty-two. Maybe she should advertise the larger cabin as a place of residence rather than a vacation spot. A small family could stay there for a few months or a year, or several years. Yes, that's what she'd do—

"*You're* in trouble, aren't you?" Addie cut into Kat's math-numbed train of thought.

She rubbed her forehead. "Nothing I can't fix."

"That isn't an answer. Sis, if you need help, dammit, we're here. That's what family's for."

"I'm fine," she insisted. "I just need to juggle a few things." And wrap her mind around selling the *Kat Lady*. If she was carrying Dane's child, the boat would be her saving grace financially.

Addie's sigh drifted over the line. "Okay, but you will let us know if you need help?"

"Mmm."

"This has nothing to do with pride," Addie went on, "so please don't—"

"I might be pregnant."

Silence.

"Did you hear what I said?" Kat asked, staring numbly at the ledger.

"I heard. Who?"

"Dane."

More silence. Then, "Kat, what's going on?"

"Things between us changed a few days ago. I—I'm not sure why. Actually, I do know why. He's—I…" Kat shot a look toward the ceiling and blew a long breath. "I've been attracted to him right from the start."

"Since he arrived?"

"Since I was thirteen."

"Say again?"

"Don't worry, I haven't been mooning over him all these years," Kat clarified. "I was just one of those dumb girls infatuated with an older boy back then. That's all. Except he wouldn't look at me. He was…" *Too busy looking at Lee.* "I was just the kid, the annoying little sister who always wanted to tag along," she said, trying for humor.

Addie didn't laugh.

Kat exhaled long and slow. "Anyway, he left the island, I grew up and met Shaun and, well, the rest, as the cliché says, is history."

"Except now he's back, living with you."

"He's back," she conceded, "but living in the small cabin." Again she pulled a deep breath. "In the last three weeks we've moved from the tenant-landlord scenario to…something else."

"That's one way of putting it," her sister quipped. "So. Explain something else?"

"To be honest, I don't know." And Kat didn't. She had no clue how Dane felt or why he'd seemed to want her as much as she wanted him in that moment. Except for the fact she hadn't had sex in too long and her hormones leapt all over the map with a glimpse of him, she didn't understand her actions at all. She wasn't in love with him. She wasn't even sure if she was in like with him. And that scared her. Shouldn't she feel some sort of emotional connection along with the physical?

Oh, for crying out loud, Kat. Just own up to the fact he's on your mind constantly. That's more than phero-mones. You're edging into love and you know it.

"Have you talked to Dane about what might be in store?" Addie said, tugging Kat back from her mental reproach.

"He'll be on board if it comes to that."

Another beat of silence. "Kat," Addie said, "can I ask you something? You don't need to answer if it's too personal," she added.

"If it is, I'll let you know."

Addie hesitated as if contemplating how to phrase her words. "Okay, then," she said finally. "Why didn't you and Shaun have more children?"

Kat closed her eyes against the memories of those days of her marriage. "Shaun had an extremely low sperm count. He was, according to the doctors, a prime candidate for infertility. So when Blake was conceived it shocked not only us, but the entire medical staff."

"Oh, sis."

"To answer your next question," Kat continued, "Shaun was against adopting other children. His theory was if it happened once, why not again?"

"But it didn't."

"No." Until his death, her husband's machismo attitude toward this one element had been a huge con-tention between them, to the point that Kat had sometimes been beyond anger and hurt. Sometimes she had truly disliked her husband's self-absorbed behavior. But she kept that to herself. "I have to go," she said, her heart aching from recollections which had in the past caused so many tears.

"I'm here, honey, if you need to talk again. Love you."

"Love you, too." And with that she replaced the receiver.

Silence dropped into the room.

One hand on her stomach, Kat remained motionless, wishing for and wishing against what might be occurring beneath her heart.

Chapter Eight

After parking the Harley in Kaitlin's carport, Dane hurried through the pelting rain to his cabin. If the weather didn't shut down the afternoon too early, he hoped to get in another round of sanding on the boat. However, first he needed to change into his work clothes and towel-dry his drenched hair.

He had donned his rattiest sweatshirt and was zipping up his new coveralls when footsteps sounded on the porch. Quickly, he pulled on the gloves he had tossed on the kitchen counter. In the bathroom, he snatched a towel. Rubbing his head, he strode over to swing open the door before his visitor knocked.

Kaitlin stood under the orange umbrella, dressed in a pink sweater, dark cords and a pair of tall rubber boots. Her brown eyes latched on to his as she held out a narrow, white envelope. "This came in today's mail."

His gaze didn't waver from her face. "Can't be mine. I haven't told anyone I'm here."

"Your name's on the envelope."

He glanced at the item between her fingers—and suppressed a curse when he recognized his mother's elegant, slanted script. No doubt his sister Felicia had done some digging as to his whereabouts before she told his parents he was on the island.

"Thanks." He slung the towel over one shoulder, then tossed the letter on the small table left of the boot mat. "Got a minute?"

"Blake's due home from school."

"He doesn't get off the bus until three, Kaitlin. We have more than an hour." Dane stepped aside. "Please," he said, softening his tone. "It'll only take a minute, I promise." With a glance at her stomach, he added, "I can make some herbal tea, if you'd like. I don't drink the stuff myself, but…" He shrugged. "I bought a few types today." While he'd taken another ride around the island, trying to sort through the enormous responsibility of his sex-starved actions that might cause her more hurt, he'd stopped in town at Dalton Foods. For her, for moments like this.

Her gaze skittered away, but she shook out the umbrella and stood it against the outside wall. Inside, he waited until she slipped out of her boots, set them on the mat before following him into the kitchenette.

From the cupboard he collected a teacup, and filled a glass with water from the tap for himself, brought both to the table in the eating nook.

Taking a chair, Kaitlin sat with clenched hands in her lap. Dane itched to warm them between his own, itched to kiss her mouth, take her to his bed. Instead, he gave himself a mental kick, found cream in the refrigerator and set the kettle on to boil for her tea.

From the small sack of groceries he'd placed on the counter ten minutes ago, he held up a garden delight of teas. "Lemon spice, cranberry-orange, jasmine, apple-cinnamon—"

"Jasmine, please."

Minutes later, he poured water into her cup. Beyond the window, the rain continued its deluge. He glanced at the hearth. All they needed was a crackling fire and the mood would be set for him to lean over, put his mouth on hers, run his fingers through her thick, glossy hair, and whisper endearments. Everything he hadn't had time to do the other day on the boat.

Next time, he thought. *We'll savor the moment.*

Next time? his inner voice scolded. *Idiot. How can you think of a next time when she might be pregnant?*

She wasn't some loose woman he'd picked up in a bar. She was a mother, for God's sake. A single mother trying to make ends meet. He had no right to take advantage of that status when all she'd done was treat him with respect and decency, giving him the space and privacy he required, but most of all giving him the chance to do something constructive with his hands.

She sipped her tea, set the cup in its saucer with a tiny clink. Her eyes met his, veered away. Again she clasped her hands in her lap. She wasn't comfortable sitting at his table. With him.

Who could blame her? He'd seized allowances from her in the most intimate way. Still, he couldn't sit here and watch her discomfort.

Reaching around the table, he laid his gloved hand over her whitened knuckles and imagined her skin cold, a sensation the fabric—and his scars—prevented him from feeling.

"Kaitlin, what is it?"

Her gaze probed his face. "Why did we do it, Dane? Why did we have sex?"

He sat back, withdrawing his hand. "Because we wanted to." With a sigh, he consigned the blame to himself. "Because I couldn't control myself around you. Still can't."

"Ditto," she whispered, and again glanced away.

Something sweet and light fluttered in his chest before he clamped the lid on the feeling and spoke more sternly than he felt. "But I won't touch you again, Kaitlin. I won't hurt you." *Because I will.* Not physically, but emotionally.

If she wasn't pregnant, he'd walk away. Walk away to keep her safe from the despondency and hopelessness that, too often, dragged him down like swamp water. He'd walk away from what he saw in her eyes this moment. Kindness and affection. Emotions that would—if he let her—evolve into the forever-I'm-yours stuff.

She straightened her shoulders. "If things work out with…if there isn't a pregnancy…. Look, I'll be honest. I don't have the time or energy for a relationship, so I'm glad we're clear on that." Her gaze darted away. Her words, he knew, belied her emotions.

Picking up her tea, she sipped, and he picked up his water. He'd let the topic drift. When she set the cup down again, her voice was strong, clear. "Where did you serve?"

"Mostly in Iraq."

"My sister Lee said you met Oliver Duvall there."

Why should it surprise him? Oliver had spoken about Lee upon his third return to the desert.

"We crossed paths a few times," Dane said. The man had died while talking to developers about a new school in a moderately "safe" area. He'd been rushed to the closest medical center—an army tent in which the wounded were sustained before they were transported to a hospital. Dane had been the command trauma surgeon in that tent. But it hadn't done Duvall any good. Moments before Dane scrubbed up, the man died.

He shoved back his chair and walked to the sink to pour out his water. "It was a long time ago."

She watched him with those all-knowing eyes. "And you don't want to talk about it."

"No."

Her gaze flicked to his hands. "Was that when you were injured? When Oliver was killed?"

"No."

"What happened, Dane?"

He wanted to tell her. He wanted to open the scar on his soul. Spew the guilt about Zaakir and how damned inadequate his doctoring skills had been when it came to a ten-year-old Iraqui orphan who, for two years, had attached himself to Dane like a son.

Talk about being a head case. Shrinks would have a field day with him. He'd put off having a family with his ex, yet he'd sheltered a homeless little boy—all because the kid's dark, survivalist eyes dared the world to defeat him. And in the end it had.

Dane leaned against the counter, crossed his arms over his chest. He knew what the stance portrayed: *Don't come near; I've shut down.* Resolutely, he reversed the direction of their discussion, and queried, "Why have you kept that boat in its cradle for four years, Kaitlin?"

Her eyes widened slightly. "Touché."

Rising, she brought her cup and saucer to the sink, carefully keeping her body from touching his, inches away. When she had set the chinaware to air-dry in the rack, she lifted her face. "I haven't had the money to fix the boat the way it should be fixed to get a fair price. When Shaun died in August the fishing season hadn't ended yet. So, the boat didn't get its annual winterizing the way it always did when he laid her up in October. I didn't know how to do it and, well…" she offered a half-smile "…that fall I had other things on my mind."

Like grief. God, could he be any more obtuse? "I'm sorry. If I could stuff a sock in my mouth, I would."

At his words, her mouth twitched. "No need for socks." The half-smile was back as she scraped a hand through her hair. The scent of spring wafted over him. "Thank you for the tea."

Dane caught her hand before she could start for the door. "How much extra for dinners at your table?"

A crease popped between her brows. "Fifteen dollars. Why?"

"Good. Count me in from now on." He dug in his pocket, drew out a ten and a five. "For tonight's meal."

She shook her head. "I can't take your money."

"Why not?"

"Because you're restoring the boat for *nothing*."

"Okay, let's clear this issue here and now. My meals are separate from the boat. It's—" He pulled in a breath at what he was about to tell her. "It's become a therapy of sorts. Besides, I'm enjoying it. Cooking, on the other hand, is not a job I'm partial to."

Suspicion flicked in and out of her eyes. She eased her hand from his when he wanted to draw her closer. "You told me you liked cooking."

"Not every day." He forced his lips in an upward slant. "After tasting your roast chicken, I'm hungry for some regular home cooked meals."

Her scrutiny set his belly aquiver. Could she suspect his reasoning? That by feeding him five or six times a week she'd gain about four hundred extra dollars a month?

"Weekends I'd cook for myself," he put in. *Or for you.*

She glanced at his forehead, as though the thought was pasted there. "I'll consider it." She headed for her boots.

Following in her wake, he grumbled, "If it were anyone else, would you have agreed without consideration?"

The boots gave her an extra inch, enough to raise her eyes to the level of his chin. "Yes." The line of her lips was firm. "I'm not a charity case, Dane."

"Good." He squelched the surge of irritation that she would see it that way. "For what it's worth, I lived and worked five years in the desert, Kaitlin. Sand and dust accompanied nearly every meal, not to mention flies and other insects. Eating at this table," he gestured to the kitchen nook, "is infinitely better. Eating at *your* table is nirvana."

He could see her balance the scale in her mind. Finally, she relented. "All right. I'll expect you tonight at six."

"I'll be there."

She went out onto the porch where the rain ran in streams from the eaves. Taking up the umbrella, she flipped it open before turning back. "Dress the way you would when you eat by yourself. These won't be special occasions."

As the thank-you meal for helping her son with his asthma had been. He gave her a crooked smile. "So you won't mind if I arrive dressed in boxers?"

Ah, at last. A lip twitch. "See you later." She turned for the steps.

He couldn't resist. "Hold on." Ducking under the umbrella, he caught her waist and gave her a hard, swift kiss on the mouth. "I lied when I said I won't touch you again. I don't want to stop touching you."

"Dane," she breathed, which nearly did him in.

He tapped her chin gently with his thumb. "Happy cooking, Kaitlin." And then he nudged her toward the steps and watched her walk away in the cheerless weather.

Back in the cabin, he picked up his mother's letter on the side table. Walking to the sofa, he sank down and extracted the single page from the envelope. Rather than the long, emotional epistles he'd become familiar with over the past ten years, she'd decided on four short sentences.

Dearest Son,

We're so happy you're on the island. Please contact us. Your dad and I would love to see you. It's been too long.

With love always,

Mom

His heart tugged at the sight of her handwriting. He imagined her gray head bent over the page, imagined her biting back tears, longing to write more, knowing he'd just discard the pages, unable to read her words of heartbreak. Still, he could not convince himself to call his parents. He could not bear the regret and distress he'd see in their eyes at the sight of his injury.

He was no longer a doctor, no longer their hero.

Whatever made him think he could be Kaitlin's?

* * *

Blake crept down the path to the boatshed the minute he could get out of the house after he'd dumped his bookbag in his bedroom.

It had been raining all week. Nothing new on the island during winter, but sometimes it just bugged him. He hated when the sopping weeds that never seemed to die even in the cold weather slapped his jeans and soaked his sneakers. His mom hated when his tennis shoes looked like something dragged out of the algae.

He wished the rain would stop, but this morning before school, the radio his mom always played in the kitchen announced there wouldn't be a letup until next Thursday. Okay, maybe that was good. With the drizzling noise, he could sneak around outside a lot better—like now. Glancing over his shoulder, he hoped his mom hadn't seen the direction he'd taken. She thought he was in the wooden fort his dad built in the big trees about fifty feet east of the house the summer before he died.

This was the second time Blake used the excuse of the fort to go outside in the rain. A twinge of shame rose. He hadn't played there for over a year, thought it too babyish. But now that he'd stashed the album in the lookout, he had a really good reason—and it would give him the chance to find out what was going on with the *Kat Lady*.

Tiptoeing along the wall of the boathouse, he heard the drone of a power tool amidst the blast of music. Finally, he'd catch whoever worked on the boat.

Amidst the noise, someone whistled a tune Blake didn't recognize. He crept around to the front where the doors stood open, and let his eyes adjust to the interior.

His mouth dropped when he saw who was up on the boat's deck.

Mr. Rainhart?

Breathing hard, Blake jerked back. Was that why the guy started eating dinner with them this week? At first Blake thought it was because he wanted to date Blake's mom, and that she wanted the same, especially the way she looked at Rainhart. Way different than any other male guest.

Bewildered, Blake stared. Was she feeding the guy so he'd clean up the boat?

He peeked around the corner again.

"Why don't you come in out of the rain, Blake?" the man said without looking his way.

Busted.

Pretending to be Mr. Cool, Blake shoved his hands into the pockets of his rain jacket, and sauntered inside and deliberately shut off his dad's radio. "What're you doing to my dad's boat?" He glared up at Rainhart, who'd come to the rail dressed in a pair of blue coveralls and a plaid flannel shirt with the sleeves rolled up to his elbows. He had big, strong arms.

"Your mother asked me to restore it." The guy pushed a pair of protective goggles onto the navy cap he wore backward. His eyes were cold as the Arctic.

Ignoring a waver of indecision, Blake went to the ladder and climbed to the deck. He stared at the patch of sanded floor where Rainhart had begun. Furious now, his voice rose. "You're changing my dad's boat from the way it was before. You're changing *everything*." He slung his hand in a half circle. "The hull, here, and in the galley—"

Rainhart's eyebrows lifted. "I haven't touched the galley." His voice was calm and it made Blake madder.

Tears pricked his eyes. "Why are you doing this? Is it because you want to move into my mom's house? So you can take over and—and ruin my life?" Like his best friend Gerry's stepfather was doing at *his* house.

"What?" Rainhart's brows bashed together. "Where'd you get that idea? All I'm doing is helping your mother. Nothing more."

"But why? We don't even know you." He glanced at the walls of the shed where his dad's tools hung. "And now you're acting like you're Mom's best friend, like you're…you're… I saw you *trying to kiss her!*"

Rainhart's face sobered. He took a step forward. "Easy, Blake. It's not good for you to get so riled."

Blake backed up. He didn't trust the guy. "What do you know about what's good for me? You kissed my mom," he persisted.

"I know you're stressed right now and that's not good for your asthma," Rainhart said, ignoring the kissing comment.

"You don't know nothing! Why'd you come here anyway? Why didn't you stay someplace else? Why our place?"

The man lifted a big shoulder. "I don't know. The picture ad in the yellow pages caught my eye, I suppose. I also liked the photos on the Web site. The cabins looked private, and that was a big issue for me. I didn't want a lot of people around."

"Why?" Curious now, Blake's trembling eased. Not once had Rainhart raised his voice. "Don't you like people? Or is it just certain people?" he tried to sneer, remembering his mom and Rainhart on the back deck that night.

"I like people fine. It's their stares and questions I wanted to avoid."

Blake's gaze fell to Rainhart's hands. "Well, what do you expect? I mean who wears gloves *all* the time?" Blake pulled a face. "Even for dinner? Dude, that's like major weird."

For a second, he thought he'd gone too far with his attitude. "Sorry," he mumbled, looking away. "I didn't mean to call you dude." He glanced back. "Mom says I have a bad habit of running off at the mouth."

"We all have bad habits," the guy said, and moved to park his butt on the railing. "But you're right. Wearing gloves is weird." His eyes seemed sad as he stared at a spot on the wall. "I tried to keep a boy from dying in a car crash."

Blake flinched at the image. Suddenly, he felt bad he'd been so mean. He was about to say something when the man removed the glove from his right hand.

Blake's eyes nearly popped out. *Holy cow.* Were those gross things...*fingers?* Repulsed and fascinated, he came closer, stared harder. His throat felt small as a needle hole. "Wow," he whispered. "Does it hurt?"

"Sometimes my hands ache when the weather's cold."

"How can you fix the boat with them like that?"

"The work helps keep the tendons nimble."

"At school there's a plastic skeleton in the lab and the hands look sorta like this, except the fingers aren't all bent and weird." Horrified at what he'd said, Blake shot the man a quick look.

But Mr. Rainhart was looking at his hand like he'd never seen it before. "Acid and fire," he said. "Makes a mess of the muscle and skin." He lifted his head. "Story time's over," he said gruffly. "Go back to the house before your mother comes looking."

Stung, Blake turned for the ladder. But before he climbed down, he had to know. "How old was that kid?"

"Ten."

Blake swallowed hard. "What happened to him? Did he live?"

Rainhart stood. His eyes were the bleakest Blake had ever seen. "No."

"Oh." Blake croaked, air squeezing through the needle hole of his throat. "That's—That's really sad."

"Yeah. It was." Drawing down the goggles, Rainhart walked to where the sander waited. A second later, he had his back to Blake and the whine of the tool filled the boathouse.

Outside Blake stood in a downpour. *That kid.* Scary images floated into his head. He hurried up the path toward the warmth of home.

Dane called Kaitlin at four and told her he wouldn't be joining them for dinner that night. "I'm leaving for Seattle shortly and won't be home until Sunday night." He wouldn't delude himself that, after Blake's visit an hour ago, the boy hadn't already described the whole unfortunate session with a plethora of flamboyant detail. Her pity when she looked at his hands, Dane could do without.

"Well, then." Her voice was pleasant, not pitying, in his ear. "Have a great weekend."

"You, too." He frowned. Had the boy kept Dane's secret after all? "I'll bring something home for Blake." Now why the hell had he said that? The last thing he wanted was to play daddy. He'd tried that once with Zaakir and look where it got him.

And if she's carrying your child?

"That's not necessary, Dane," she said, slicing off the thought. "He's got everything he needs. But thank you for thinking of him."

"Does he like to read?" Dane persisted, no longer caring if the boy disclosed the reason and condition of his injured hands. The reason for buying something became a matter of simply because.

"Sometimes," Kaitlin said. Was her voice a little breathless? "He's read all the Harry Potter books, but lately he's more interested in writing in his notebook. His teacher assigned it as a personal project for her students called Island Life."

"Interesting." After today, Dane had no doubt he'd have a starring role in the boy's entries.

"I think it's a good project." Her voice lowered as if she didn't want her son to hear. "Something's going on with Blake."

Oh, yeah, something's going on, all right. Me. Dane recalled the boy's accusation about a kiss. He had no idea where that came from. For damn sure, it wasn't in the boathouse. On the afternoon in question, Blake had been at his aunt's house.

Drawing a hand down his bristly cheeks, Dane wondered if he should find another place to stay—perhaps on the other end of the island—like the kid suggested.

Out of sight, out of mind?

Absence makes the heart grow fonder?

Dane scowled. What the hell was the matter with him, mulling over a pair of old axioms?

"Dane?"

"We'll talk on Monday, Kaitlin."

"I'll miss you," she whispered.

And just like that his heart did a backward flip. He closed his eyes. "Same here."

He hung up before he walked out the cabin door and into her kitchen and kissed her again and again and again.

"Isn't he eating with us tonight?"

Kat elevated a brow as her son entered the kitchen and cast a sidelong glance at the table set for two rather than three. She knew exactly who *he* was, but asked anyway, just to draw attention to Blake's manners. "Excuse me, but don't you mean Mr. Rainhart?"

"Yeah," her son muttered.

"Then say so, Blake." Setting a bowl of spaghetti and meatballs on the table, she added, "He's going to Seattle for the weekend. Did you wash your hands?"

The boy rolled his eyes. "Duh. I always do."

"Please don't speak to me that way."

"Sorry."

"Accepted. Let's eat."

They sat in their respective places, and Kat dished out the whole wheat noodles. Blake dug for more meatballs than sauce. "How come you never told me he was fixing the *Kat Lady?*"

So that's what incited this mood. "Because…" How to begin? "I knew you'd worry that I was going to sell the boat."

"Are you?"

"I may have to." She wanted to say, *There aren't many renters during the winter months and my savings are running low*. But she wouldn't put the burden of her finances on her child's shoulders.

"I don't want you to sell it." Blake's expression was one of worry. "The *Kat Lady* is Dad's boat. She's part of the family."

Kat hesitated, then said, "Uncle Colin wants the boat for his fleet, so if he buys it she'll still be in the family…in a way." The moment she'd incurred the unexpected expense of the washer and the water pipe, she'd been thinking about Colin's offer. The time had come to face the fact that no matter how careful she was, in the past forty-eight months her savings were eroding.

Blake picked at a meatball. "Uncle Colin won't care about the boat the way Dad did."

"It shouldn't be collecting cobwebs, son." To quote Colin.

Her son's silence was answer enough. His head remained down throughout the meal until he suddenly said, "I saw Mr. Rainhart's hands today."

"His hands?"

"Yeah. Without the gloves. He showed me and they're really gross and—"

"Stop right there, Blake," Kat interrupted. With a deep breath, she marshaled her words. This was Blake and, for some reason, Dane had taken him into his confidence. "If Mr. Rainhart told you something in private, please respect that."

"You don't want to know what happened?" her son asked, astonished. "Why he always wears gloves?"

"No, I don't want to know." She rose to clear the table. *What I'd rather have is Dane's trust.* This was, no doubt, about the child suffering on his watch. "Have you finished your homework?" she asked instead.

"No."

"Then do so now."

Grumbling under his breath, Blake left the kitchen.

Kat filled the sink with soapy water. She tried to ignore the wave of hurt. Dane had kissed her, had sex with her, but he hadn't trusted her with the one thing she suspected tormented him enough to hide in a cabin in the woods—and away from his family.

She didn't know whether to laugh or cry or get downright angry that he would unload his plight on her child.

Automatically, her eyes searched beyond the window above the sink for the cabin's lights among the trees. Of course, all was dark. Tonight, while he was sleeping in Seattle, she'd be sleepless here.

The semi-pun wasn't lost on Kat.

She turned away with a sigh.

Chapter Nine

The end of March approached with blustery ocean winds and low-flying rain clouds that parted every few days for snippets of blue sky and a placid sun. One morning Dane ran into a problem in the boatshed.

On deck, the aged cowl ventilators required replacing. He'd recognized the problem when he'd first opened the doors of the pilothouse and caught the musty scent of mildew. Why Kaitlin's husband hadn't changed the ventilators to the more conventional and easily manipulated "mushroom" style was a mystery. Finances perhaps? Or maybe he'd been reluctant to tackle a job involving several hours work. Whatever the case, Dane wanted modern vents, with water separators that prohibited wave spray or rain from entering the galley and causing dry rot. Fresh air below deck was vital while you were on the water for long hours, or on an overnight trip.

Although he'd already purchased the new equipment, installation would go quicker if he had an extra hand; the only name that came to mind was Zeb Jantz. Years before, Zeb had flawlessly renovated the kitchen, bathroom and screened in the back porch of Dane's childhood home.

The old fellow had semi-retired a year ago, but agreed to help Dane on this sun-patched Thursday morning.

Surveying the *Kat Lady* side-by-side, the two men stood with their thumbs hooked in their back pockets.

"You done good, boy," Zeb observed. "Fine job of sanding." Nearly sixty, the man was hale and fit as a twenty-year-old, with big shoulders, trim waist and work-hardened hands. Without hesitation, he climbed the ladder to peer over the rail. "You got a knack for renovating boats," he commented. "Not everyone knows how to bung screw holes that well."

Yesterday, Dane had spent an hour filling new screw holes with various sized teak plugs matching the deck. He couldn't wait to apply a coat or two of varnish and have the floor shiny as a minted penny. Then show it to Kaitlin.

Zeb climbed back down. "Kat's going to be one happy lady, and it's about time, too."

"I hope so," Dane said.

The old guy peered over. "And I hope you're not charging her an arm and a leg. After what she's been through, she needs a break."

Dane kept his expression neutral as he unhooked his safety glasses from the wall. "You mean her husband's death," he said casually, avoiding an answer to the arm-leg charge. The deal between Kaitlin and him was no one's business.

"I don't mean to speak ill of the dead, but Shaun

shouldn't have gone fishing that last time. He knew about the pending storm. He also knew his cousin took shortcuts on the water."

"Shortcuts?" A chill sliced through Dane as he lifted one of the ventilator boxes to his shoulder and started up the ladder. All the summers he'd spent on his grandfather's fishing boat, Dane remembered the old man's maxim. *If you're gonna be a seaman, never disrespect the ocean 'cause she'll take you first chance she gets.*

Zeb hoisted the second vent box. "He'd pile the ropes instead of coiling 'em. Wouldn't sweep the deck entirely clean of crabs and junk after a wave wash. That sort of thing."

Dane bent over the vent. "Are you saying Shaun didn't care enough to say anything to Colin?"

"You had to know Shaun." Zeb studied the deck's job site for a moment. "His daddy used to run this boat the way his daddy before him. But Shaun wasn't interested in fishing or taking the business over. Instead, he went to college, thought he'd be a marine biologist."

"Yet he married Kaitlin and came back here." And became a fisherman.

"That he did. He loved her, don't get me wrong. But…"

"He wanted to do more with his life," Dane supplied. Doctoring overseas, he had been where the real action was. So he thought. He glanced at the older man. "How do you know all this?"

Zeb grunted. "A handyman's like a barber. People unload their worries on us while they're watching us work on their projects. 'Sides, I've been in the business too long not to hear a thing or two."

"Or talk about it," Dane muttered, fitting the vent over the hole from where the old one had been extracted.

"Huh. Well, gossip isn't my thing, but I will say this. I'm glad you're doing the work for Kat. However, mark my words." His voice had a clipped edge. "If I hear you're taking advantage of her, I'll take you for a long walk off a short pier." His knees cracked as he squatted across from Dane and smiled. "Understand?"

"Loud and clear. But who made you her warden?"

Zeb's eyes were dark and keen. His mouth remained sealed.

"You can't be interested in her," Dane said, incredulous.

"Not as a man. And we'll leave it there."

Three lengthy seconds ticked by as each man waited out the other. First to relax, Zeb said, "If you must know, and you will eventually, this island's too damned small otherwise—her mother is someone I care for."

Dane let out a long breath. Ah. The old guy was playing stand-in daddy. Okay, he could deal with a man's protective instincts when it came to the people he loved. Hadn't a few protective—and admittedly, *possessive*—instincts reared up at the notion that this fit, silver-haired man might have romantic intentions toward Kat?

"Got it," Dane said.

Zeb's mouth twitched. "Figured. So, want to get this done?"

"On one condition." Dead serious, Dane stared at the old man. "We do not discuss Kaitlin again. Ever."

"Deal."

Friday at six, Kat answered Dane's light knock on the back door. "Hey," she said with a soft expulsion of air when he stood in front of her, dressed in black trousers and a white long-sleeved polo shirt. As usual—with a distance of only eighty feet between their doors—he'd forgone any outerwear.

"Hey," he replied with a hint of a smile.

Say it, Kat. "I'm not pregnant," she blurted.

His blue eyes blinked slowly. The smile dimmed. "You're not?"

She shook her head. "I had my period."

"Okay." One word, two syllables. His gaze touched her stomach. "Okay," he said again, and she detected relief, the same relief she'd felt last week—on the heels of a sense of loss.

"I wanted to tell you tonight because—because we're alone."

His dark brows skipped skyward. "Alone?"

"I meant…" God, could she be any more blatant? "What I mean is that Blake is at Lee's for a sleepover and you're my only company for dinner. So…so certain little ears aren't around."

Four beats of silence. Then the corners of his mouth turned up and he stepped over the threshold. "Yeah?"

Kat moved to close the door, anything to keep from looking at that sexy grin and imagining what his mouth could do on her skin. Turning toward the kitchen, however, she realized her mistake when he hadn't moved and she nearly put her nose into the open collar of his shirt. "Oh!"

He caught her elbow. "There we go."

"Sorry, I wasn't paying attention."

Stepping aside, he let her pass. "You look very pretty tonight, Kaitlin."

Lord, what made her think he wouldn't notice she'd taken fifteen extra minutes in her closet, digging out her favorite burgundy skirt and mustard-colored sweater? Was she that naïve to think a man like Dane wouldn't detect a woman's subtle preening when normally she wore a variety of colored jeans most days?

"Smell good, too," he added as they entered the kitchen.

She had no come back except for a polite, "Thank you." And a mental reprimand to never again be so ridiculously obvious. "Please," she said, "take a chair. I'll bring the casserole over in a second."

He remained where he was. Two feet from her elbow. "Can I help?"

"Sure. Salad's in the fridge."

He removed the bowl while she donned thick mitts and pulled the chicken and broccoli dish from the oven.

When everything was set and they were seated at the long rectangular table, he said, "Had I known we'd be eating alone I would've brought some wine. Better yet, I would've made *you* dinner."

In his cabin. Where they'd be isolated rather than alone. And the bed twenty feet away. She stopped the images there and offered him the salad, holding the bowl while he scooped greens onto his plate with wooden tongs.

"Aren't you eating?" he asked, when he'd filled his plate with three helpings of her casserole.

"In a minute." She wanted to say something profound. That this was a first, a man sitting alone with her, dining in her kitchen. That she admired the growth of his hair over the past weeks, and liked its color even better—sort of the golden Brad Pitt look.

By now she was so accustomed to seeing his hands covered that it no longer looked incongruous or odd for him to wear his tight skin-hued gloves to the table. Or anywhere else for that matter.... Now she knew what the fabric concealed thanks to her son.

She looked away.

"Something wrong?" He set his arms on either side of his plate. The sleeves of his shirt were rolled to just below the elbow and the sight of those sinewy, hair-dusted forearms jolted a current through her stomach.

Say it, Kat. Say what's on your mind. "This is nice," she began.

A crooked smile appeared; the tension from his forehead eased. "Agreed." He passed her the casserole dish. "Eat, Kaitlin, because I'm not touching my fork until you do."

She did as requested and took a bite. He followed suit murmuring, "God, I love your cooking," after several mouthfuls.

"I suppose anything would taste good after Iraq."

"You're right. But this…" He filled his mouth again and she watched his lips, those sensual lips, move as he chewed. "Mmm."

Warm with pleasure, Kat reached for her water glass, sipped. "Tell me about it," she said. "About the war."

He shrugged.

Okay. She could understand his silence about a place she'd been witness to only through the camera of a TV journalist, because Firewood Island had had its share of mourning. Long story short: war was hell.

She decided to take a different tactic. "Why did you join the military?"

"Why does anyone?" he countered.

Strike two. "Dane."

He glanced over.

"If you'd rather not talk about your time there, just say so. I don't mean to pry. I'm simply interested in…you."

"I don't want to talk about my time there."

Deflated, she stared at her plate. "Okay, then."

With a gust of air, he set down his fork. "What do you want to know?" Tension stretched the skin over his cheekbones, compressing his mouth, so sexy moments before, into a stark line.

She shook her head. "Not like this."

"Like how?"

Kat placed her knife and fork on her plate, pushed her chair from the table. "With your hackles up. With distrust in your voice. I'm not the bad guy here, Dane. Just so *you* know."

He caught her hand before she could rise. "I'm sorry, all right?"

So was she. More than he knew. She thought they had something between them. They'd made love. She trusted him to repair her boat. Or was it all a goofy fantasy she'd built because of loneliness and because he'd been her first crush at thirteen?

She tugged her hand free and walked to the sink where she unloaded her meal into the trash in the cupboard beneath.

His chair scraped across the hardwood. "Damn it, Kaitlin. I don't know what you want."

Turning, she stared at him. "Guess that's two of us. I'm in the dark as much as you when it comes to this relationship—if it's even *a* relationship." *Why are you afraid to show me your hands?*

He walked toward her, stopped close enough that she could smell his skin. Wearily, he said, "Ah, Kat. There's so much you don't know about me." His thumb caressed her chin. "I've been broken and I'm not sure if I can be put back together again."

The abbreviation of her name on his lips liquefied her insides. "I'm not afraid," she whispered. "It doesn't matter to me if you're the same as you were before you went over there. Who you are right now, that's the man I want to know, who I want to—"

He moved closer, placed his hands on her hips. "Want to what?"

To love. "To be with, which—" her mouth wouldn't stop "—which I've wanted from the time I was thirteen!"

His brows leapt.

Omigod. She couldn't believe her silly, foolish mouth.

With a half-snort, he eyed her askance. "Get out of town. You did not."

"Believe it. I had the biggest crush on you, but all you did was toss calf eyes at Lee."

He threw back his head and laughed—a laugh she loved instantly—and the tension flung like a slingshot from the room. "Kat, Kat." His eyes sparked amusement as he pulled her close. "It's a damn good thing I gave Lee the calf eyes, don't you think? She and I were the same age. But you... you were..."

"Her bratty little sister, I know. And yes, had we hooked up, you could've gone to jail. Which never entered my silly girl mind. All I wanted was for you to look at me. Just once."

"I'm looking now," he said softly.

"Mmm. And I'm no longer thirteen."

His blue gaze darkened, dipped slowly to her chest pressed against his snowy shirt. "No," he said. "You definitely aren't."

The house phone rang.

Kat's first thought was Blake, but when she lifted the receiver, it was her mother. "Hey, sweetheart, are you up to having a couple of visitors this evening?"

Kat glanced at Dane watching her from the other

side of the worktable. How had he gotten over there so fast? "Actually, Mom, I'm sort of—"

"Oh, just put the coffee on," Charmaine interjected. "We'll be there in fifteen minutes." *Click*.

"—busy." Kat stared at the silent phone in her hand. "Gee, thanks for letting me finish, Mom."

"Trouble?" Dane asked.

"Seems my mother's bringing company over as we speak and she wants me to put the coffee on." Kat drove her fingers into her hair. "Grrr! I could just shake her. She's always popping by as if I have no life!" Her gaze swung to Dane. "Please stay. I need a buffer so I don't end up stomping off into the woods or something."

His mouth quirked. "If I stay, your mother might get the wrong idea."

"God, I hope so," Kat said, irritated. She went to the table and began clearing the dishes. "She's convinced I'll end up an old widowed woman in my nineties. Ha. She should talk. She's gone through two husbands and a guy no one has a clue about."

Dane took the casserole dish to the worktable. "What guy is that?"

"My father." Kat dumped the remainder of the salad into the compost bin next to the trash. "Apparently, she doesn't know who my father is or was, or so she maintains. But Lee, Addie and I figure she knows *exactly* who he is. She just won't tell. It's—" Kat dittoed the air with her fingers "—Mom's closet secret."

Dane began loading the dishwasher. "Is she seeing anyone now?"

"Possibly. Probably. The thing is, I'd always thought Cyril Wilson was my dad, too, because he married Mom eleven months after I was born, so I figured they were just slow in getting their marriage act together. But, he's Addie's dad. Biologically."

"Addie," Dane said, studying the pot in his hands. "She was about three years younger than you, right?"

"The baby of the family." Kat scraped the rest of the casserole into a plastic container for the refrigerator.

"I didn't know your mother had married three times."

"She didn't. For some reason my father entered the picture between her first husband, Lee's dad, and her second husband, Addie's dad. Trouble is, Mom never married *my* dad—or told anyone who he was."

Dane leaned a hip against the counter. "Someone must have known him."

"Oh, I'm sure they did. They just didn't know my mother had a clandestine relationship with him."

"Maybe he was already married."

"It's crossed my mind. Except Mom's been so closed-mouthed about his identity, that having the guy in the neighborhood would've driven her crazy with worry."

"You think he's been off the island all these years?"

"I do."

"And he's not Lee's daddy?"

Kat grunted. "Apparently that scum left when my sister was three—and two months before I was conceived." She shot him a fake grin. "Seems he'd made another little nest in Oregon, even had a son there. No, he's not the invisible man."

Dane's gaze was steady. "How did you find out?" he asked, so gently Kat's eyes stung.

Blinking hard, she faced the dishwasher and punched On.

"Heyyy." From behind, Dane's arms were warm and

strong. Bending his head, he pressed his cheek to Kat's. "I'm here."

Turning in his arms, she buried her face in his throat. "When I was sixteen, I got Mom's permission to donate blood because the medical clinic was running low. I knew Lee was type A, because she'd donated the month before. I also knew Mom was type O from all her previous donations. One thing about Charmaine, she's never refused to give blood. I think it's because her dad needed a transfusion when he was a young man and it saved his life."

"And Addie?" Dane asked against Kat's hair.

"I found out two days later that she's type O as well." Kat raised her head. "I'm type AB negative." His brows leapt. She sighed. "I love my mother, Dane, but in this I resent her deeply. I don't know what that says about me. I had a counselor once tell me I'm lacking an emotional puzzle piece to carry a grudge so long." Her smile trembled. "Maybe he's right."

"To hell with the shrinks," Dane said roughly, then kissed her. The kiss lingered, deepened.

When a knock sounded from the front door, they jerked apart.

"She's here," Kat said in a hushed voice.

"And I should go." He glanced at the window with its white, flower-patterned sheers, the window facing the circled front drive. A line cut between his dark brows.

"Don't worry. They can't see in." She followed him into the mudroom, resenting her mother's intrusion more than ever.

He stroked her cheek. "Thanks for dinner. Delicious as always." Their eyes held, and she thought, *Not as delicious as you*.

When she closed the back door, the knocking at the front door grew insistent. For a moment, Kat stayed in the unlit mudroom. Breathing slowly, deeply, she gathered her emotions. Emotions she'd laid wide open to a man she barely knew, but felt such a strong kinship with it almost frightened her.

She walked through the house. She'd told him things about her past and he hadn't shrugged them off. Hadn't said, *"Let it go, Kat. No point fretting over something you can't change."*

Funny how she recalled Shaun's words as if he'd just spoken them, rather than thirteen years ago after they were engaged to marry. At the time, his nonchalance hurt, but then she'd realized Shaun's motto was, quite simply, to live life as happily as possible and not to worry. Things aren't as bad as you believe.

He had a point. But she would've liked his support, nonetheless.

Putting a smile in place, she opened the door.

Charmaine stood in the glow of the porch light, immaculate as always, dressed in a trim chocolate-colored jacket and matching pants, her graying red hair coiled into a fat, casual bun.

"Hello, dear." She stepped aside so Kat could see the tall, slim woman waiting behind. "Remember Mrs. Rainhart? She's come to visit her son."

Chapter Ten

Kat disguised her surprise. When had Dane's mother become *her* mother's friend? Yes, Mrs. Rainhart was once a regular at Charmaine's hair salon, but since retiring Charmaine had devoted her time to babysitting her grandchildren, baking treats and putting up preserves for the families of her three daughters. Just last week, Kat pulled the last jar of Charmaine's homemade plum jam from the pantry shelf.

"This is what retirement is all about," she'd told Kat and her sisters last Christmas. Flitting from child to child, she'd played pat-a-cake with Addie's young son Alexander, and Barbies with her girls Becky and Michaela, nuzzled Lee's baby girl Olivia, and built a mini plastic town with her stepson Danny and Kat's son Blake.

There was no denying Charmaine loved and doted on her grandchildren. Nor had it gone unnoticed that she relaxed more around the little ones than with Lee, Kat and Addie. With her daughters, Charmaine often seemed on guard.

As she was now, standing on Kat's porch.

"Aren't you going to invite us in?" Charmaine asked, thrusting a container of raisin tarts into Kat's hands.

"Yes, of course." She moved off the threshold as the two women entered. "Hello, Mrs. Rainhart. It's been a while."

The woman stood about two inches taller than Charmaine. Her white hair was thick and straight and tucked behind her ears. There were laugh lines around the same deep blue eyes Dane possessed.

"Please," she said, "call me Yolanda." The creases highlighted her smile. "I think we're well beyond the Mrs. Rainhart stage, don't you?"

Kat liked her immediately and returned her smile. "Come in," she said, heading for the kitchen. "I'll put on some decaf."

Worried she and Dane might have missed some proof they'd been in the kitchen minutes before, Kat quickly scanned the counters and table; only tidiness greeted her guests.

"Where's Blake?" Charmaine demanded, taking a side plate from the cupboard and setting out several raisin tarts, while Yolanda took the chair Dane used a half hour ago. "I know how much my grandson loves pastries, especially these."

Kat got her best china from the dining hutch. "He and Danny are having a campout for the night."

"Goodness, not in the middle of winter," Charmaine exclaimed.

"No," Kat assured, "they're setting up in Lee's living room with the pup-tent Rogan bought last summer."

"Oh, thank heaven. March is way too wet and cold. They'd come down with pneumonia or worse."

As though Kat or Lee would allow their sons to sleep on the damp ground. She might have known her mother wouldn't let a remark about parenting skills go by the wayside. Charmaine thought Kat should be more vigilant with Blake because of his asthma. When Shaun built the play fort in the trees, Charmaine fumed to Kat, *"What if he falls or gets winded climbing the hill?"* Twenty feet up a gentle slope was Mount Everest to Charmaine.

"Dane used to love camping out," Yolanda commented. "When he was a little boy, he'd drag the kitchen chairs into the living room and drape blankets all over to make caves and forts." She laughed the laugh of a young woman delighted with her little boy.

"Blake used to love doing that, too," Kat said, smiling.

Charmaine took the cream from the refrigerator. "Must be a boy thing."

"Perhaps," Yolanda said. "But Dane was like his dad and grandfather in so many ways. He loved hiking and fishing and scuba diving, all the things Ben did in his younger years. We were often amazed at the similarities between Ben and Dane—far more than Felicia, our biological child." Yolanda chuckled. "She is not the outdoorsy type. Not the way Dane is."

Kat's hands stilled. She'd forgotten Dane was adopted. *Why* had she forgotten? *Because it was never an issue for him.* Nor, evidently, for his parents. Certainly not the way it had been for Charmaine and Addie's father when Kat's youngest sister became pregnant at seventeen.

Yolanda smiled. "You didn't know my son was adopted?"

"Yes, but…" Kat glanced at her mother. "You're so…so open about it."

Something akin to amusement flickered in the other woman's eyes. "Shouldn't I be?"

"Of course. I meant—" The knot in Kat's shoulders loosened. "You and Dane obviously have a very special bond."

"We are close. Or we were." Sadness stole across Yolanda's features and Kat wanted to rush to the phone and call Dane back to the house. But the older woman's eyes brightened again. "When I couldn't have any more children, Ben and I put in an application to adopt. We fell in love with Dane the second we saw him in his little bassinet. Right from the beginning, he made us happy and proud—more than we ever could have imagined. Both our children have."

Are you getting this, Mother? Kat thought, refusing to glance across the table. *She has no secrets from her children.* "Has Dane ever…?" Unable to put her question into words, she rubbed her brow. "Forgive me. It's none of my business."

"Wanted to know his biological parents?" Yolanda asked, guessing Kat's question. "He's always maintained that we are his parents, no one else. However, we were never secretive about his adoption with either of our children. We prepared Felicia before he came home, and then we told Dane the moment he was able to talk and understand. When he was three or four he'd tell company, 'I'm 'pecial cuz I'm 'dopted!' Again she laughed. "People thought he meant *doped,* so we always needed to explain his pronunciation."

Kat couldn't tear her gaze from Dane's mother. *We were never secretive with our children.* The woman's words reeled around Kat's brain until she could barely breathe. This mother held no shame about her inability to give birth. Instead, she spoke of her dilemma freely and with love for the baby she had chosen to bring into her home, to raise as her own.

Turning slowly toward Charmaine, Kat was startled to see her mother watching her reaction. *She knows what I'm thinking.* A fury rose in her chest. She wanted to demand, *Stop hiding the truth and tell me who my father is!* As always the question that had plagued her for almost two decades followed: *Do you even know?* That scared Kat more. What if Charmaine really didn't know? What if she couldn't admit she'd been so promiscuous at a time in her life as to not be able to distinguish one lover from the next?

But no. Lee had been three when her father walked away from Charmaine—and Kat had been born a year later.

Instinctively, she knew her mother would not have brought a string of men into her house where Lee toddled.

Until she was sixteen, Kat believed Addie's father was her parent, but then came the day of the blood discrepancy and her entire life had turned upside down.

Coffee poured, she sat across from her mother at the kitchen table, and forced a smile.

Yolanda took one of Charmaine's pastries. "Hmm," she said, chewing a tiny bite. "Blake's a lucky boy to have a grandma who bakes like a chef."

Kat watched her mother beam. Charmaine said, "One day you'll be doing the same, Yolanda."

The other woman smiled. "If it happens, it happens. But Felicia seems married to her social services career and Dane…" Suddenly she set down the pastry, bent her head and shielded her eyes with her hand. A cough masked a sob.

"Yolanda?" Charmaine reached for her friend's free hand.

"I'm sorry," the other woman whispered.

"Mrs. Rainhart." Kat rose. "Can I get you a glass of water?"

The woman lifted her head, wiped her eyes. "Yes, please. That would be nice."

Kat went to the fridge for the cold pitcher she kept there.

"Thank you, dear," Yolanda took the dewy glass. "And I apologize. You see, I know my son has been staying here for the past month. I haven't seen him in almost four years. Not after his divorce and not when he was injured. He won't let us come near him. To this day, I don't understand it. I know the divorce tore him up and the injury…" A gusty sigh. "I wish he'd let us help him get through whatever he thinks he's protecting us from." She glanced at Charmaine. "I asked your mother to bring me here on the pretense of seeing Dane." Her worried gaze wove back to Kat.

"Mrs. Rainhart—" she began, heart aching for mother and son. "Yolanda, I'm not sure he…" *Wants to see you.*

"I know." The older woman stared into her cup. "My husband warned me. 'Let him be,' he said. 'Let the boy come on his own.' But a mother…" Her eyes welled again. "A mother just can't sit by and watch her child *hurt.*"

No, Kat thought. *A mother wants to take her child's pain onto herself.* Hadn't she wanted to rip away Blake's asthma three weeks ago, insert his struggle for air onto her own lungs? When Shaun died, hadn't she wanted to load her son's agony onto her heart, liberate him from the debilitating grief of losing his daddy?

Yolanda removed a tissue from her purse in her lap, dabbed her nose. "Would you please tell him I was here? And…and to come home. We won't meddle or ask questions, I promise. But we need to know he's okay."

"He is," Kat assured. "He's fine. He's working to restore my boat," she added, hoping to set the woman's mind at ease.

Charmaine looked across the table, astounded. "Are you selling it, then?"

"It's too early to say."

"But Kat—"

"Mom, stop. This is not about me, okay?" To Yolanda she said, "I'll tell Dane about your visit."

"Thank you." Sensing Kat's tension regarding Charmaine, Yolanda climbed to her feet. "And thank you for the coffee. You're very sweet to listen to an old woman's woes."

"We're all mothers here." Kat darted a look in Charmaine's direction.

Yolanda touched her cheek. "For a young woman, you're very wise. I'm glad my son is here with you." To Charmaine, she said, "I'll wait for you in the car."

When the other woman had left and the front door clicked closed, Kat gathered the cups and pastry plate and carried them to the sink.

"You were nice to Yolanda," Charmaine said.

How else had her mother expected Kat to act? "She's hurting."

"I don't know why her boy is acting this way."

Kat turned. "What way, Mom?"

Clutching her purse to her waist, Charmaine lifted her chin. "I don't like your tone."

Kat sighed. What was the use? They'd danced around the topic for eighteen years. "I'll see you out."

"Maybe I should see myself out," Charmaine retorted.

"Mom, can we not do this tonight?"

"What? I didn't do anything. You're the one with the attitude. It's because of what Yolanda said about her boy's adoption, isn't it? About not having secrets."

Kat walked into the living room. At the door, she turned. "Yes, it is. But I really don't want to discuss this tonight. Goodnight, Mom." She kissed Charmaine's cheek. "Drive carefully."

"I love you."

"I know. I love you, too." She opened the door and waited for her mother to pass.

"Can I come back tomorrow to see Blake?"

Kat made an effort to breathe calmly. "Can we take a rain check? I've got some things to do this weekend."

"Fine. If you'd rather not see me…"

"Mom—"

"Okay, okay." She went out onto the porch, into the cool night air. "I'll call you Monday."

Arms crossed against the chill and holding the door open with a hip, Kat waited until Charmaine traversed the stairs and walked to her car, then she offered a small wave.

This thing between them would never end.

Because you can't let go.

Back in the kitchen, she washed and rinsed the cups and plate; cleaned and prepared the coffee pot for tomorrow's breakfast. When all was in order, she checked the stove clock. Eight-fifty. Under the blanket of night, a hush stole through the house. Sometimes, while Blake slept over at Lee's or Addie's, Kat looked forward to an evening alone. But tonight, with the dark pressing the windows, impatience flowed into her bones.

She went to her bedroom, but couldn't convince herself to prepare for bed. Upstairs, she stood on the threshold of Blake's room, and stared at the little piles of clothes on the floor and chair and dresser. She inhaled his youthful scent. Down in the living room, she tried to get comfortable on the sofa, but found herself flicking through channel after channel on the television.

And all the while, Dane's lack of desire to search for his biological parents harassed the back of her brain.

How could he disregard his family? She'd spent her entire life wondering about her ancestry. They were so different, yet so alike.

Clicking off the TV, she tossed the remote aside and headed for her jacket in the mudroom.

She needed the cold ocean wind on her face. She needed to escape the whirling questions in her mind, the tangle of emotions surrounding Dane. She needed—needed—needed—

Flashlight in hand, she slammed out the front door and jogged down the dark, weedy path to the boatshed. The *Kat Lady*… She'd sit on the *Kat Lady* and pretend she was on the water where the cares of the world drifted to the ocean bottom. She'd pretend she had a father—and a mother who loved her enough to tell the truth.

She'd pretend Dane wanted what she wanted, and that she wasn't alone in her quest after all.

Yes, for an hour she'd pretend, and try to ignore the tears wetting her cheeks.

Dane had the boathouse's dusty old radio tuned to the familiar metal music station from Seattle. Once, eons ago, he'd enjoyed easy-listening and/or country, but living a half decade in the Mediterranean changed all that. Now, he preferred racket—as he called it—to drown the recurring images of wounded and dying soldiers. Of Zaakir.

Tonight, however, the noise cloaked other images, those of Kaitlin in her kitchen, smiling, her hips swaying gently in that wine-colored skirt. And that sweet voice as she told him of her nameless father. The scent of her, something akin to flowers and wind and sunshine, still lingered in his nostrils.

He became aware of her, gradually, above the noise of screeching guitars and crashing drums.

Both hands pressed to the collar of her jacket, she stood inside the shed's side door, staring back at him.

"Hey," he said, vaguely aware of the coveralls he'd changed into after dinner. He walked over to the wall shelf and shut off the radio. Silence shot in like a mortar shell. "Company gone?" he asked, setting his brush on the can of white paint nearby.

She walked toward him. "You're painting the hull white." Not a question, but a statement with an edge.

Her tone didn't concern him. Her spiky eyelashes and flushed cheeks did, however. "You've been crying."

Quickly, she palmed her face. "No, I'm just…"

Dane tipped her chin toward the light. "Why were you crying, Kaitlin?"

She jerked away. "It's nothing. Just stupidity."

Okay, he wouldn't press the issue. He was here, if she needed an ear. He returned to the paint pail, hammered down its lid and wrapped the brush in plastic, ready for the morning. Kaitlin remained several feet away, observing his every move. When he rose again to grab his weary army jacket from a nail near the door, she followed as he flicked off the lights and led the way out the side door, before slamming home the deadbolt.

The sea wind riffled his hair and crept under the open panels of his jacket. He welcomed the cold. Around Kaitlin, his blood ran too hot, too intense.

They started up the path, arms brushing now and again. She hadn't spoken another word since he questioned her tears, but after twenty steps he succumbed to his emotions, and caught her hand and they continued up the path like lovers strolling in the moonlight. He almost laughed at the notion. She was on a mission, her stride matching his, her eyes focused on the house through the trees.

When they reached the graveled circle, he asked, "Are you expecting more company tonight?"

"No."

"Good." And then he led her around the carport to the path angling from her deck to his cabin.

Halting in front of the porch, he said, "I want to make love with you, Kat. I've wanted it more than anything in my life. However, if you're not ready, say so here and now and I'll go inside alone."

One moment stretched into two, then three. He thought she'd turn and go to her house—or tell him to go to hell. Instead, she said, "Did you know your mother was part of my company tonight?"

Had Kaitlin tossed a pitcher of ice down his back, the heat in his blood couldn't have cooled quicker. "What did she want?"

"To see you." She paused. When he remained silent, she asked softly, "Why won't you visit your parents, Dane?"

His jaw tightened. "I'll see them when I'm ready."

"Your mother is very worried about you."

He debated what he should say next. Like her son, she was curious; wanted to know, to *see*.

"You can't hide forever," she said quietly. And then she glanced at his hands, at his ever-present gloves, making a statement without words. Her eyes lifted, held ten long seconds.

Dane wanted to do exactly as she'd said. Hide. Hide in the cabin. Hide from the world. But most of all hide from her. "Didn't Blake tell you what happened?" he asked roughly.

"Should he have?"

Dane winced. The last thing he wanted was Blake hiding things from his mother.

Scraping a hand over his hair, he said, "I'm sorry. I had no right telling Blake anything. At the very least, I should have come directly to you and explained the situation."

"Yes, you should have. My son is a very impressionable eleven-year-old and you're a man who is a paying guest at my B and B."

Except he'd kissed her, and made love to her. Well. Apparently, he'd read her wrong. He wasn't her lover; he wasn't *anything* to her. What he was, was money in the bank.

"Point taken. And this," he said, yanking off one glove, then the other, and tossing them onto the porch. "This is why I conceal my hands."

Mesmerized, he watched her reaction. Any second she would turn in disgust. Or stare in horror.

He watched for the slightest change in her expression, in her demeanor. His heart beat hard, one-two-three-four… His blood thumped in his ears. Still, she remained motionless, not voicing a sound, simply observing what he displayed: the puckered mess acid and fire made of skin; the pale, ghastly scars.

How could she not notice his gnarled knuckles? How bulbous the fingertips where the skin congealed at each end? Was she surprised his left pinky remained the only finger with a nail?

Christ, he thought assessing the damage through her eyes. No wonder he wore gloves 24/7. Hell, even *he* was repulsed, and this was *his* body.

"Piece of work, isn't it?" He couldn't suppress the taste of bitterness as he turned his wrecked hands palm up where ridges replaced the lines in skin stretched tight as canvas. "Bonus is…the tendons in most of the fingers and my left thumb are still intact, so I have some movement." He demonstrated, wiggling the digits slowly.

"Oh, Dane."

Her voice sounded watery, as if she spoke from the depth of the sea. He looked up, tried to discern her meaning, but she was reaching for his ruined hands and gently taking them in her own. And when she bent and laid a kiss in his palm, his heart stopped. Fascinated, he watched the slow progression of her head as she moved across each hand. The injury had left little sensation under the skin, but he knew her lips touched the knuckles, fingers and wrist, because in the silence he heard the soft, tender sounds of her kisses.

He thought he might die at her feet. "*Kat.*"

Lifting her head, she placed his hands against her breasts, then up to frame her damp cheeks. Her heart stood in her brown eyes, and he knew he'd fight to his last breath for her if the situation surfaced.

"My love," she whispered, rising to her toes, rising to his mouth while her hands pressed his against her cheeks.

His throat contracted as the air in his lungs vanished. She didn't pity him, she… Was it possible? Was it possible this strong, beautiful woman, this gentle, vulnerable woman…loved him?

Dane's heart hammered so hard he was certain she'd see the motion under his jacket. *Kaitlin.* She was a wonder, a hope, a gift he hadn't expected.

He tried to speak, to enunciate the emotions beating in his chest. Instead, he took her hand in his, led her up the porch steps, past the cast-off gloves lying on the wooden floor, and into the cabin where his bed waited. The time for words would come later. Tonight he'd speak with his body.

Chapter Eleven

The second the door closed, Kat felt herself lifted into strong arms. Without removing his boots, he walked across the meticulously clean floor and down the hallway to the bedroom facing the wooded hillside. She knew the room inside and out; she'd furnished and decorated it years ago.

Dane shouldered his way through the door, and in three paces laid her carefully on the soft, patchwork quilt with its homespun squares of gardens and woods, bees and songbirds.

He didn't flick on the lamp to dispel the moonlight glowing through the window. Slowly, Kat's eyes adjusted to the darkness, and clung to his. He hovered above her, hips at her thighs, arms next to her on the pillow.

"Dane," she said softly. She lifted a finger to his mouth, traced his bottom lip. She smiled at the quickening of his breath. "Do you know how often I've thought of this moment since that day you sat on your Harley in the pouring rain?"

He dipped his chin, slowly.

"You know?" she asked, surprised.

"I've thought of it, too. A thousand times."

She took her time mulling over his statement. He was as attracted to her as she to him.

He said, "This won't be like the boathouse, Kaitlin. This is going to be exactly how we've been fantasizing."

A trill of electricity heated her belly. "And how's that?"

"Slow, fast, everything you want for as long as you want."

Oh! Her thighs liquefied. "What about you?" she rasped.

"I'll take what you want to give." His head lowered. "This is for starters." His mouth took hers.

Wet, mobile, slow, hot. Sensations rocked Kat to her toes. Oh, but the man could kiss. And kiss. And kiss.

When he finally eased back, stars pelted her insides.

"I can't wait for the main course," she said.

Through the obscurity, his teeth flashed white. "We need to get rid of our boots and clothes," he whispered. The bed dipped as he sat up and took her feet in hand, removing first one rubber boot, then the other and letting them fall to the hardwood. *Thump—thump.* By the time he reached for her skirt, she'd undone her belt and had the garment pushed to her knees.

"Kaitlin, hold on." Staying her hands, he flicked on the bedside lamp. "I want to see you." His gaze traveled her bared tummy, pink cotton underwear, thighs—back to the underwear. Bending, he set his mouth there and— *ohhhhh*—blew a long hot breath against her.

"*Dane.*"

Before she could say another word, he was kissing her again, his tongue dueling with hers until she ached and clutched his back, wriggled out of her skirt, and wrapped one leg around his hips, while the other worked its way between his thighs.

"Kat," he gasped as he wrenched away. "I need to feel you. Now." Kicking off his boots, he unsnapped the coveralls, tore his sweatshirt over his head.

Somewhere beyond her wanton haze, she marveled at the deftness of his hands as they dispensed with his clothing. She hated that he felt embarrassed about a disfigurement caused in a war to protect their country. To Kat those scars were icons of his profound gallantry.

When he reached for his boxers, she reached for his hands. Her eyes rose to his as she laid his imperfect palms against her sweater, where her heart pounded. "First, take off my clothes, Dane."

The lamplight bronzed his shoulders and shadowed one cheek. Two more scars cut across one of his biceps, another ran from his ribs into the thick tawny hair on his chest. She wanted to kiss each injury. She wanted to heal his soul.

His mouth worked as his eyes darkened to match the night outside. Slowly, he took the hem of her sweater between his fingers, and tugged it up and over her head.

"The bra," she coaxed when he remained motionless, staring down at the last garment. "Touch me the way I want you to."

She waited several seconds, and when he still hadn't made a move toward her, she did it for him, taking his hands and putting them on her shoulders.

"Kat." His voice was sandpaper. "I haven't touched a woman like this, without the gloves, since before…"

She placed her hands over his and climbed off the bed. Pressing her belly against his boxers, she said, "I know, honey. But this is me and I love your hands the way they are." Tears blurred her vision. "I love *you,* Dane. I won't be melodramatic and say I've always loved you, because that wouldn't be true. But I do now. I've been falling in love with you for a month." Her fingers curled around his. "I don't expect anything in return. The words are for me. You can take them or leave them. But this…what we're doing tonight…is for us. You and me." She gave him a watery smile. "Now slip off my bra and touch my breasts. Please."

An expression of wonder crossed his face. "You," he said, "are a gift."

She rose to her toes and gently pressed a kiss to his mouth. "Do it, Dane."

He did. Bit by bit, he moved his hands down her arms, as she lowered them, taking the straps along. When they circled her biceps, he inched down the cups. Kat watched his face, the awe in his eyes as he followed the route the bra journeyed. When it was about to drop from her breasts, he looked up and saw her watching him.

"Almost there," she said softly.

"You're the most beautiful woman I know, Kaitlin. You have a heart as big as the moon. You've given me back my confidence."

Bending his head, he kissed her tenderly, then slipped the bra down until it fell to her waist. His wounded hands lifted and touched her with a reverence that made Kat want to curl up and cry. Never had a man been so gentle, so loving. Shaun had loved her, but his technique in bed had been different. And for that she was glad. She wanted no comparisons tonight.

She captured Dane's fingers, kissed each bulbous tip, then tugged his boxers past his erection.

"Kat," he growled when she kissed him there.

In one swoop, he lifted her onto his bed and caged her between his arms, his weight pressing her into the mattress. She loved the feel of him, his strength, the careful way he touched her face and breasts and far below.

The next few minutes held her in thrall as he loved her with his hands and mouth and when they both panted, she prepared him from the box he'd bought after the first time in the boathouse.

But before he entered her, before he made them one, he said, "You don't expect anything from me, least of all the words. But you hold my heart, Kaitlin, the way you've held these—" He displayed his right hand with its damaged fingers. "You know me as no one has. And you still want me."

"I do," she whispered. "Come here." Cupping his bristly jaw, she brought his mouth to hers. Soon the only sounds within the room were those of sighs and rustles and two souls merging.

Dane lay on his back, his arm around Kaitlin, his thumb leisurely stroking the soft inside of her elbow. She lay curled against him, head on his shoulder. The pliant muscle of her calf was a sweet weight on his bony shin.

He'd turned out the light an hour ago, and now lay listening to her languid breathing as she slept. Except for the spots where they clung to each other, the sweat had dried on their skin.

He loved her scent, and the way her thick, straight

hair bunched against his jaw. Every night, he wanted to crawl under the covers, smell that spring-fresh perfume her body emanated.

They had made love twice, and the pleasant fatigue stealing across his muscles pulled at his mind. For years, he hadn't felt this relaxed, this content—or this in love. Because he loved her. *Loved. Her.* With every ounce of his being.

He couldn't remember feeling this way about another woman, not even his ex-wife. But he wouldn't let the truth shame him; sometimes people married for what they believed were the right reasons, when in reality the reasons were all wrong. Sometimes immaturity and inexperience were part of those wrong reasons, as they had been for him.

Kaitlin stirred. "Dane?"

He turned his lips to her forehead. "Here, sweetheart."

"Haven't you slept yet?"

"Dozed a little."

She stretched like a cat, caving her spine against his hand, pressing the soft heaviness of her breasts into his side. Between his legs, he roused.

"Mmm," she murmured with a small moan, touching him.

He caught her hand and brought it to his chest. "You need to rest. Morning will be here before you know it."

"I don't want to sleep." She kissed his jaw, journeyed to his mouth. "I want you."

"Kat…"

"I love when you call me that."

Pleasure streamed through him. "That makes me very happy."

Snuggling against his arousal, she teased, "Can I make you happy some more?"

He chuckled. "You already have. See for yourself."

"Oh, I do see." Laughing, she climbed on top of him. "We're not wasting one second of that."

"Okay, then," he said, and grinning took her breasts gently in his hands. "You've convinced me."

Later, as he held her in his arms and set his mouth against her hair, he dared. "You've never asked how I was injured. Why?"

"You'll tell me when you're ready." Shifting, she looked into his eyes. "And if you never want to explain, that's okay, too. I don't need you to bare your soul in order for me to love you, Dane. What's past is past. I'd rather deal with the here and now."

He turned on his side, faced her on the pillow. After tucking the hair on her cheek behind her ear, he let his hand drift to her nape, his thumb stroke the line of her chin.

"I love you, Kat. More than I can say. When I look at you, when I hear your voice or touch you, my heart gets so damn big I think my chest might burst."

She remained quiet; it gave him courage. "I wish I'd come back after you grew up. I wish we'd had the last ten years together. However, I'm not foolish enough to think things would've been different or that there wouldn't have been problems. Back then I was a young, cocky doctor, thinking I could save the world single-handedly."

"I've done a few stupid things over the past decade as well," she said.

"But not like this." He drew in a deep breath. "On my first tour overseas, I met a triage nurse. Phoebe was five years older and, at the time, had the same goal. To serve our country. Six months later, we married. Suddenly, she wanted to return stateside and start a family. I didn't. Instead, I sent her back and stayed for another tour. I kept making excuses not to come home. Long story short, I let Phoebe down. Two years later, we divorced. I'm not proud of what I did concerning my marriage, but I will say I'm very glad she remarried and now has a child."

"Dane, we all make mistakes—"

He rolled away and got out of bed. "You don't understand." He grabbed a pair of blue jeans from a drawer in the dresser.

Kaitlin came to her knees. "Then tell me." She reached for his arm as he zipped the pants. "Don't hold back. I won't run away."

He stared at her kneeling on his bed, unaware of the sight she made, naked and lovely in moonbeams streaming through the window. "I don't know why I started this tonight."

She stilled. "Started what?"

She thought he meant their lovemaking. "Tonight was supposed to be only for us, Kat. Not a shrink session." He turned and walked out of the room.

"Dane—"

He heard her scramble off the bed, thump, curse, and then her bare feet pit-patted after him down the hallway.

"Dammit, Dane. Don't you dare leave this cabin." She flung in front of him as he reached the kitchenette.

She'd yanked on his sweatshirt, the neckline drooping off one small smooth shoulder, the sleeves dragging below her fingertips, the hem hanging mid-thigh. Heat roared through his chest and down into his groin. If she didn't move out of the way, he'd take her right here on the floor, without preliminaries, without fuss.

"Kat, I need to get out of here."

"Then I'm coming with you." She planted her hands on her hips. "I'm not leaving you."

The words *get out of my way* strangled behind his tongue. "Please," he managed. *Please, let me go. Please, I'm not good for you. Please, I can't do this.*

Slowly, she raised her palm and set its warmth against his cheek. "It's okay," she whispered. "You're okay."

Closing his eyes, he hung his head, and felt her hands cup each ear as she pressed her brow to his chin.

Time evaporated. He lost count of the seconds, the minutes—perhaps the hours—they stood like that in the dark. Her, holding his head; him with his hands dangling at his sides. He swallowed and swallowed again. Finally, the words came....

"Sixteen months after Phoebe left Iraq I went with a medical team to medicate a refugee camp full of desperate, but kind people. They'd suffered incredible brutalities by insurgents." Clenching his teeth, he bit back a shudder. "One boy lost his entire family, raped and shot in the middle of the night. God knows how he escaped, but the next day he hooked up with refugees traveling the road. At night, he slept on the ground under a filthy blanket... survived on scraps tossed his way. He was nine years old."

Kaitlin's fingers massaged Dane's scalp above his ear. He concentrated on the sensation, but the memories continued to bloom, large and vivid and full of horror.

"I'm here, honey," she whispered, sensing his distress. "I'm not going anywhere."

"His name was Zaakir," he continued. "His skin had blisters and infections. I ended up taking him back to our base camp, gave him a bed, food, care and began proceedings for a stateside family to adopt him. Trouble was he wanted to stay with me. And, well...after almost a year, he'd become like a son." He laughed humorlessly. "The great Dr. Rainhart who wouldn't have kids with his wife."

"Sometimes things happen for a reason."

Silence extended. "Yeah," he said finally. "They do. In ways you don't expect." The morning he'd driven Zaakir to a village in the province of Diyala, intent on buying the boy a few new clothes, they'd found themselves in the crossfire of insurgents.

Kaitlin listened, simply listened as he uttered his memories. For that alone, he loved her. He went on with the story, misery in his soul. "My car..." He inhaled hard. "My car was hit." God Almighty. He felt and heard it all again.

The explosion, the screeching metal...

Zaakir's cries...

His own body slamming to the ground...

"The car flipped. I was thrown out the driver's door. But Zaakir...I heard him moaning. I tried to crawl under the wreck. Battery acid was dripping on his face. Fire was everywhere. I put my hands out to shield Zaak..." A violent tremor rivered through Dane. "He died in my arms, Kat. I—I couldn't do a damn thing."

"Shh," she soothed, slipping her arms around his neck, rocking him where they stood. She didn't speak, just held on.

After a long while, after the shivers quieted, he drew back and swiped the heels of his hands across his damp cheeks. His focus cleared, adjusted to the darkness. She watched him, concern etched between her lovely brows.

"Sorry," he said. "I haven't done that before." In all the years of his profession, he'd never broken down, not when death in the desert and the third world was a common occurrence. *Except you didn't expect it with Zaakir; he'd been your symbol of survival.*

Had Dane been able, he would've laughed. *Symbol.* God, he was still an arrogant son-of-a-bitch. The kid had yearned for a family with Dane as his dad but, no, he hadn't been prepared to give Zaakir that. All Dane had wanted were the accolades, the pats on the back....

"We're damn glad to have guys like you here."

"We couldn't have done it without you."

"If it wasn't for you..."

Intuiting his disquiet, Kaitlin shifted, tucked herself against his side, and slipped an arm around his waist.

"Kat—"

"Let's go back to bed, Dane," she said softly. "You're safe now."

Yes, he thought. With her he'd found refuge, he'd found home. He went willingly.

Kat dug a half carton of eggs from the kitchenette's refrigerator, put them on the counter and began preparing a plate of scrambled eggs. The coffee gurgled in the percolator, its fragrance enticing and delicious. She poured a cup.

She'd wakened an hour ago while the night still tussled with daybreak, and when orange and pink seeped through the trees, she'd left Dane sleeping.

A smile hovered on her lips. He'd been curled around her like a big, warm bear, his arms holding her close, his legs twined with hers. Four years was a long time to wake alone, and this morning she reveled in the feel of a man at her back, a man she loved.

And she loved Dane. Heart, body, soul. Last night he'd stripped away the layers covering the festering agony he'd carried for two years. A milestone, she knew, but then in the midst of his grief, she'd accessed her own milestone.

"'Mornin'." Behind her, his voice was jagged as bark.

She glanced over her shoulder, smiled. Bare chested and sockless, he stood in gray sweats that hung soft and loose from his hips and profiled his sex. Any residue of the previous night, of his sorrow, had vanished. His eyes looked clear, his face rested. When she'd brought him back to bed, she had loved him slowly, tenderly; then held him until he slept.

Scratching his chest, he wandered toward the stove where she stirred the eggs.

His arms with their dark gold hair, circled her waist. "I like what you do to my clothes," he said, nuzzling the hair from behind her ear.

She'd donned the sweatshirt from the night before. "It was the only thing I could find that was warm."

"Mmm. Anything under it?" One hand skimmed her thigh.

Giggling, Kat sidestepped. "You men. Always thinking with your morning stuff."

"Stuff?" Amusement lit his eyes. "I wouldn't call this," he glanced down, "stuff. This is a damn decent woo—"

She shoved the breakfast plate into his chest. "Time to eat."

Feigning chagrin, he took his eggs to the table and waited until she joined him. "Looks like it'll be a nice day," he said, glancing at the widening arc of blue above the trees.

Kat watched him take a bite, watched his sensuous lips move as he chewed. Unable to stop herself, she leaned in and kissed those lips. "'Morning," she whispered against them.

In the pale dawn, his whiskers were the color of oakwood and incredibly sexy. His dark gold hair edged over his ears and down into short shaggy sideburns. He'd run his fingers through the crown, driving locks this way and that. One draped his forehead and touched the black line of his left eyebrow.

His eyelashes were thick and black—the kind women selected from stores. At thirteen, she had found those eyelashes surrounding his blue-blue irises the most attractive feature she'd seen on anyone, never mind a boy. Back then she'd considered him gorgeous but unattainable. Today, he was a very potent man, a man she loved and, who, yes, was attainable, but would he let her heal his sorrow? *Could* she heal it?

"What is it?" he inquired when she continued to stare without eating.

"I'm thinking that I need to change." *And be careful with my heart.*

His brows bunched. "In what way?"

She poked at her eggs. "I need to stop fussing about my mother and her secret lover. And I need to stop hanging on to the *Kat Lady.*"

"What brought this on?"

She raised her head. "You."

"Me?"

"Last night, your mother said you were never interested in looking for your biological parents, that you'd always felt the Rainharts were your parents."

"True," he said slowly. "My natural parents probably made the choice to give me up long before I was born. Why make a hornet's nest out of the past?"

"You were never curious?"

Dane shrugged. "Sometimes. But overall it wasn't

important to me, Kat. Not the way it is with you. Besides, my circumstances were different. Your mother deliberately withheld information. My mom never did. She told me from the time I was three. She even listed me with some child find registry in case my real mother decided to look for me one day. When I was eighteen I deleted my name from the list."

In her lap, Kat picked at a cuticle. "I envy your detachment."

"Don't." He covered her hands with his, stopped their fidgeting. "You need to do what you've got to do, honey. I'm the last guy you want to model yourself after. God, Kaitlin, look at me. I can't even get my life in order over something I *knew* could happen. Hell, that I'd *seen* happen a dozen times."

"With other people."

"Yes, with other people—"

"Not with your own."

He shook his head. "That's just it. Zaakir wasn't my own. He was an orphan I took under my wing. That's all. I was trying to get him adopted so he'd have a family again. Then when he died…"

"You lost it."

"Yes. I'd seen so much pain over there, maybe he was the straw that broke the camel's back. I honestly don't know."

Kat did. "It's because you loved him like a father."

"Damn it," he said, withdrawing his hand from hers. "Don't make this into some kind of hero worship."

She shoved back her chair. "Hero? Dane, don't you get it? After what you did, you *are* a hero. And, for what it's worth, this isn't worship, it's reality. No matter what you say, you loved that child the way I love Blake. Your emotions after his death are the same as any father who's lost a child. Whatever you do, don't minimize Zaakir by saying he wasn't yours. He was in every way that counted." Because she wanted to erase the haunted look in his eyes, her hand found his fist on his thigh. "Just as you are to your parents," she said softly, "and they are to you."

He pushed his half-eaten plate of eggs away. "Don't put me up on some glorified pedestal."

A heavy silence fell.

She said, "You really don't believe in yourself, do you?"

"Would you?"

"Yes! Look how far you've come, Dane. My God, you survived a war. You journeyed home. You've taken on the repairs of my boat. You've—"

"Fallen for you?" he asked.

She sat back, stunned at his tone. "Even if you hadn't," she said, and her heart broke. "You did come here to move on. At least admit that."

Plate in hand, he rose and looked down at her. "I love you, Kaitlin. God knows, I do. But to move on the way you're hoping… I'm not sure I can do it. Now or ever."

He carried his dish to the sink and scraped the egg remnants into the trash, before walking down the hall to his bedroom.

Kat sat blinking in the sudden piercing sunlight that hit the window. After a moment, she got up, took her coat from the row of hooks by the door, and let herself out into the crisp, cool morning. She'd go back later, when he wasn't there, and get her clothes. Right now she needed to crawl off in a corner and soothe her wounded heart. And not cry. She definitely would not cry.

Chapter Twelve

Dane heard the front door of the cabin quietly open and close. He kicked the dresser with his bare foot, welcoming the pain that shot up his ankle and shin.

Dammit.

What the hell was the matter with him, treating Kaitlin like that—and after the night they'd had? What kind of man made love to a woman, then gave her an emotional punch in the gut?

A complete and utter jackass.

With a guttural sigh, he drove his hands into his hair. He had to go to her, had to apologize.

Seems you're always apologizing to her. Can't you ever get it right the first time around?

Frustrated, he scanned the room, but his gaze kept returning to the bed with its rumpled sheets and quilt, the head indentations in the pillows. One step and he had the nearest pillow against his face, inhaling the scent of her hair.

Kat, he thought, helpless against the onslaught of loss. He wanted what she wanted. To make a life together, be a family. The surprise of that came out of nowhere. He'd never wanted a family, always thought his work was the mainstay of his life, and now…now, he could think of nothing else except that he yearned to etch out a future with Kat and her little boy.

The thought of Blake wrenched Dane's heart. The other day in the boathouse he hadn't been kind to him; instead, he put the run on the kid. *Story time's over,* he'd said when Blake got too close with his questions about Dane's hands.

Lowering the pillow, he stared at his twisted digits clenching the quilt. *When are you going to stop letting them rule your life?*

Kaitlin was right. He had to move on, make a concerted change in his life.

Last night she'd told him he was safe. Safe with her. Why couldn't he believe it? She hadn't been repulsed by his injury, hadn't run screaming into the hills. No, what had she done? Kissed his grotesque flesh over and over, let him stroke his hands, his fingers across her most private places. A symphony of sensation, playing across her body, *in* her body.

The memory thickened his blood. He replaced the pillow, then walked to the foot of the bed where her yellow sweater hung haphazardly from the bedpost. Her bra and panties—how had he missed they were pink?—lay on the floor under the windowsill. Inside out, her corduroy skirt sat in a heap beside the dresser.

He wandered the room, gathering up her clothes.

Folded neatly, he took them to the kitchenette where he found a plastic grocery bag and put the clothes inside. He'd give them to her as soon as he showered and shaved.

Providing she opened the door when he knocked.

Kat was at her office desk tallying the month's expenses and wondering if her allowance was sufficient to buy the new sneakers and jacket Blake needed when she heard the *tap-tap* on the mudroom door. Her heart skipped. It could only be Dane. Barely forty minutes had passed since she'd left the cabin, came home and stood in the shower pinching back tears. She'd been determined to get her mind off him, and office work was her only avenue—even though she'd added the amount in the debit column three times with varying results.

Tossing down her calculator, she went to answer the door. At first she was puzzled; the deck was empty. Had she heard a knock? And then she saw the plastic sack bulging with her clothes. As she bent to retrieve the bag, the roar of his motorcycle broke the morning silence.

He was heading out, leaving her. He'd set her clothes at the door and was leaving.

Wheeling around, Kat ran through the house. She flung open the front door, rushed across the porch just as the Harley's taillight flashed red among the trees, and then disappeared.

Dizzy, her head felt so dizzy. He hadn't waited for her to answer the door. He hadn't cared enough to say, *I'm leaving*. Had last night meant so little to him? Worse, how could she have misjudged him? She returned to her office, sat in the chair, put her face in her hands. All the words they had said to each other... All the things they'd done together...

He had been with her through every move, every kiss and touch. He'd been *there*.

Only in your mind, Kat.

No!

She jumped up so fast the motion thrust her chair into the wall behind. Her fingers shook as she unlocked the bottom drawer and dug through her files for the cabin's master key. *Hurry, and find out for sure.* Outside, she ran up the path, took the cabin's steps in two bounds before driving the key into the lock.

His loafers sat on the mat, his fatigue jacket hung on the hook. The magazines and books were stacked on the coffee table and the big stainless steel thermos he used for coffee still sat on the drying rack by the sink.

Relief closed her eyes. He hadn't left. He'd gone for a ride somewhere, maybe to see his folks. She could only hope.

Her shoulders slumped, then rose again on a long deep breath. A whiff of his shaving lotion pervaded her lungs, and she smiled.

"When you're ready, Dane," she whispered to the stillness. "You know where to find me."

Backing from the threshold, she pulled the door closed. A turn of the key and the cabin was as he'd left it. A spring to her step, she walked through the woods to her house. If it took forever, she'd wait for him. He *would* move forward, she had to believe that. It's what people in love did for each other. They didn't bail out or run away. They faced difficulties side by side, they supported one another.

Dane wasn't Shaun. He wasn't boisterous, or as quick to anger as to laugh, instilling his presence on everyone around. No, Dane was the quiet pool hidden in the forest, a pool Kat wasn't about to give up—for both their sakes.

Riding the Harley, Dane looped Shore Road twice around Firewood Island before finding the nerve to turn into his parents' driveway south of town. The last time he'd been to the little Craftsman house where he'd spent his childhood was shortly after he and Phoebe married.

The changes were evident: a new cedar-shake roof; green siding with white trim rather than the all-white look; and his mother's honeysuckle hedge along the sides of the property reached high above his head.

He pulled in front of the door of the detached garage, and cut the motor. Removing his helmet slowly, he remained astride the bike listening to the cooling tick of the engine as he scanned the home of his youth. He and Felicia had tumbled on the grassy front lawn. He'd experienced his first kiss with Lee Tait on the porch steps. Kaitlin had been twelve then, a skinny girl with long dark pigtails. That day she'd tagged along after Lee as usual, and was in the house with the rest of their friends. He recalled how she'd whacked open the screen door, and gasped. *"Eew—you're kissing her?"*

The recollection lifted the corners of his mouth. Her horrified expression hung clear as a photo in his memory, memories she'd uprooted with her gentle touch and soft voice through the night.

The front door opened; his mother blinked down at him. "Dane," she cried, cupping her cheeks. "Oh, Dane."

He swung off the bike.

His silver-haired dad appeared at Yolanda's shoulder. A small white poodle yapped from behind the old man's heels. "Shush, Critter," he warned the little dog. "Well, now, son," his dad beamed. "Aren't you a sight for sore eyes."

"Mom, Dad," Dane greeted. "Got the coffee on?"

Laughing, his mother hurried down the steps. "Oh, honey. I'm so, so glad you're home." Hooking an arm through Dane's, she asked the man on the porch, "Isn't it fine, Ben? Isn't it fine that our boy's home?" She steered them into the house, into the kitchen where nothing and everything had changed. Old rose-patterned linoleum and knotty pine cupboards; new glass table and poodle pup.

Watching Critter prance around his father's ankles, Dane thought of the black mongrel that had been like a quiet shadow when he lived in this house. Still, he couldn't resist patting the little canine sniffing his boots. "Not like old Bard, this one."

"Not in the least." Ben Rainhart replied as he sat on the edge of a stool next to the butcher island. "So, you here to stay, son?"

"Ben!" Yolanda brought over the sugar and cream. "Give the boy a moment, will you? He just got in the door, for heaven's sake."

The old man eyed Dane. "Yes, he did. But he's been on the island a month. I figure he's made up his mind by now."

"Don't listen to him," Yolanda said. "Your father's been antsy since Lissa spoke with you on the street."

"And," his father said, voice full of disappointment, "you refused to see us."

"*Ben.*" Yolanda glared at her husband. "Give it a rest, already."

But Dane shook his head. "Dad's right, Mom. I should've come right away."

"You had your reasons." She patted his forearm. "You don't need to explain them to us."

Dane looked at his dad. "Except I do." That's why he'd come, wasn't it? Kaitlin had asked him why he was hiding, well, it was time to crawl out of his cave, stop this emotional fear. These were his parents. They knew him in ways no one could. They'd seen his flaws and understood them since he was a baby.

He set his hands on the table. "You know why I was in that Boston hospital."

"You were burned," Yolanda said, though her tone hinted regret at Dane's decision to not allow her visitation rights. "We heard what the rebels did to that town."

He tugged off his gloves, spread his hands on the table. "This is why I've been away."

His mother let out a cry. His dad murmured, "Ah, dammit, boy," and looked away.

For a long moment both parents sat in shocked silence. Finally, his father took one of Dane's hands, studied the destruction and gently ran a blunt-tipped finger over the welts and puckers. "I know a great reconstructive sur—"

Dane jerked away. "See, that's why I didn't let you or Mom come to Boston, and why I didn't tell you I was back on the island. I know surgeons, too. Damn fine doctors who can do a world of patch work, but all that reconstruction won't return the sensation in my fingertips. It won't prevent the unsteadiness." His eyes held Ben's. "I'm done with medicine, Dad. I'm done being a doctor. It's never going to happen again. I know *you* want me to go back to that life. You want me to hope, to think positive thoughts, to regain that drive to never say never. You've always wanted it—and I appreciate that in you. It made me strive to be the best, to reach for the highest rung." He watched his father's face. "But I'm no longer the best. The quicker you understand that, the better it'll be for all of us."

"But the guy I know—"

"Ben." Yolanda clasped her husband's shoulder. "Leave him be."

Dane shoved back his chair and rose. "I need to go."

"But, you just got here," his mother protested. Her worried gaze darted between the two men.

"I'll be back," Dane assured her.

"Please don't mind your father." Yolanda gave her husband a look of frustration. "He's worried, is all."

Using the table as support, the elder Rainhart stood as well. "Who the hell wouldn't be, Yolanda? This is our kid. He's worked too hard to throw it all away."

With great care, Dane pushed in his chair. "God, Dad. Listen to yourself, then look at this mess. *Really look.*" He stretched out his fingers in an attempt to straighten each digit. Dexterity had improved slightly with work on the boat, but the gnarled twig manifestation remained. How could his dad not see the truth? How could he not see those nubby fingertips shaking like miniature dried bulbs swinging in a wind?

His mother's eyes clouded. His father's mouth was a severe line.

"Dane," Yolanda said quietly. "What can we do?"

He offered a half-smile, a truce. "Just accept who I've become."

Kat didn't see Dane again for the rest of the weekend. A hundred times throughout the two days she was tempted to walk down to the boathouse and see how the work progressed.

Oh, who are you kidding? she thought, flapping clean

sheets over her bed Monday morning. *It's him you want to see*. And talk to and kiss and…a gazillion other things.

Steamy warmth slid through her lower belly. The past two nights she'd missed him fiercely. She missed his arms and his touch. She missed his weight on her body, his tenderness and the words he whispered for her ears only.

But she wouldn't beg. She had done that with Shaun when they disagreed—which, in all likelihood, had driven him further away.

With Dane she would let him choose. Her…or his fear. When he made the choice, she would be ready, whatever it was.

"Mom!" Blake slammed through the front door.

"In here," she called, bagging her pillow with a freshly laundered case.

His feet thundered down the hallway and she wondered if he'd removed his boots. Last night it had rained and a damp mist shrouded this first morning of spring-break.

Blake swung around the doorjamb. "Dane's changing *everything!*"

Kat came around the bed. Her son's short hard breaths, the sweat on his pale brow alarmed her.

"I went down there! Mom, did you hear what I said? He's changing a bunch of stuff on the boat."

"I heard, Blake." She lifted his chin. No doubt, he'd run rather than walked the hundred-yard trail from shore to house. "Did you take a puff when I asked this morning?"

He wrenched free. "*Mom, jeez!* He painted over the *Kat Lady*'s name."

"He's giving the hull a new coat, which it's needed for several years, Blake."

"No, no. He's changing the name to *Lady Kaitlin*."

Kat frowned.

"Did you tell him to do that, Mom? Did you?"

"Of course not."

Blake grabbed her hand, tugged her down the hallway. "C'mon. You gotta tell him to change it back. You need to tell him to stop everything, or he's going to ruin Dad's boat. Man, it won't even *be* dad's boat anymore."

She stopped at the top of the stairs, a chill skipping over her skin. "What changes are you talking about, Blake?"

"You know, like the new ventilators and stuff."

"New ventilators?" she asked stupidly.

"Jeez, Mom. Don't you ever go down there and check on things? He put in these new vents, even had Mr. Jantz help him."

"Mr. Jantz? How do you know?"

"Dane told me like five minutes ago."

She stared at her son. Zeb? Working on the boat? Why on earth hadn't Dane told her of the added expense, an expense she could not allow him to absorb?

"I'll get my coat," she said, and hurried down the stairwell to the mudroom.

On Kat's heels, Blake said, "I'll come with you."

"No, I'd rather you stay here and let me handle this."

Mutiny lined his mouth. "If it wasn't for me you wouldn't even know. You never go down there."

Oh, but she had gone down there. Kat felt her skin warm. "I think it's best if I talk to Dane first, all right?"

"Okay. But what if he gets mad?"

The question startled her. "What makes you think he'll get mad?"

Blake averted his face. "Sometimes he sounds mad. Sometimes, he looks at me like I'm not even there or…or he doesn't like me."

Kat's first instinct was to deny her son's words, but she'd heard the anguish in Dane's voice when he'd talked about Zaakir. She'd witnessed the damage to his body, his spirit. The first night Dane had come to dinner, he'd tried to reach out by allowing her son to carve the roast chicken, but then Dane had shut down when Blake asked him about his hands. And she'd seen the disappointment in her child's eyes when Dane wouldn't talk about motorcycles that day in the carport.

Still, she knew the underlying reasons, and so said, "Sometimes Dane feels really sad. Remember how you felt when Daddy died? You didn't want to see your friends, but they kept phoning and wanting to talk?"

Blake looked at his feet. "Yeah. But that was different. Dad was never coming back." Anger flashed in the boy's eyes. "I don't want Dane taking over Dad's boat like...like it's his!"

"He's not taking over," Kat stressed, shrugging into her jacket. "He's repairing the *Kat Lady* because of an agreement we made. Nothing more."

"Yeah, right. He wouldn't do it unless he wanted to buy it."

Dane buy the boat? The thought hadn't crossed Kat's mind. And, yet... He knew boats, he'd had experience working on a fishing trawler with his grandfather. And then there was the end to his medical career. The *Kat Lady* would be the perfect alternative.

Kat looked at her son, waiting for her answer. She gave him the truth. "He's never mentioned buying it, Blake. But if he does I know he'll give the boat special attention."

"He's trying to be like Dad, isn't he?"

Kat's heart turned over. "Oh, son. No one will ever

be like your daddy. He was a very special man *because* he was your father."

"Then why did you kiss Dane on the deck that night?"

He'd seen that? Before she could respond, Blake continued, "Do you like him better than Dad?"

"No," she said. "I like him differently." To bring the point home, she asked, "Do you like one cousin better than the rest?"

Blake shook his head. "I like them all the same. Well, sort of the same. I mean Danny is different than Becky and she's different than Michaela and..." His brow furrowed. "Is that what you mean?"

Kat smiled. "It's exactly what I mean. Your dad will always have a special spot in my heart. But so do you. And so does Dane. You're all in my heart, Blake, just in different ways. Make sense?"

"I guess."

"Good." She touched his chin. "Now, take your sheets from the dryer and put them on your bed. I'll help you make it after I talk to Dane."

"Don't forget to make him change the name back."

Kat moved to open the mudroom door. "I sort of like *Lady Kaitlin*."

"But it's not the name Dad picked."

She stopped. "Okay. Remember when Aunt Addie met Uncle Skip and you found out Becky was your cousin, too? And then Aunt Addie married Uncle Skip and now little Alex is Becky and Michaela's brother? That's what happens when life continues on. Remember last year when Aunty Lee decided not to fly her plane because she wanted to stay close for Danny and little Olivia?" Kat set a hand on Blake's shoulder. "Honey, even though our feelings for Daddy won't change, he'd expect us to make new friends and move on."

Blake hung his head and chewed his lip. "Sorta like Dane's our friend?"

"Yes, like that."

He thought for a long moment. "Okay," he said, turning to leave. Then, "I guess he *is* making the boat pretty nice. Dad would probably be real happy."

Kat smiled. "I think so, too."

"Do you think they'd be friends if Dad was alive?"

"Yes," Kat said softly. "I do."

"Then I wanna be Dane's friend, too."

So do I, Blake, Kat thought when her son left. However, first she needed to get some things straight with the man in question—such as those beyond-her-budget costs he had accrued.

From the moment the boy ran out the door, Dane had expected her—and now here she was, stepping into the boathouse.

Setting the paintbrush in the pan he held, he walked over and silenced the radio and Metallica. The hush threatened to disclose his bopping heart. God, she looked good. Those red jeans were fantastic and the way that white denim jacket fit to her waist... Grimy as he no doubt appeared, he longed to stride over, haul her into his arms and kiss her lush mouth.

Her lips parted as though she detected where his thoughts had wandered, and she quickly looked toward the nearly refinished boat. "Blake said you've altered parts of the *Kat Lady*."

Her clipped tone rather than her statement brought

Dane back full force. "It needed new vents and a new engine."

"Did Zeb Jantz help with some of the reconstruction?" This time her gaze returned to him.

"He did."

"My current budget isn't conducive to Zeb's fees, Dane."

Frustrated that she'd think he pawned the expense onto her, he said, "Zeb worked for *me*."

"Except I own the boat."

"As in 'don't forget who's boss'?"

She pushed at the swathe of hair across her forehead. "That isn't what I meant."

"No? I thought we agreed on the reasons I'm restoring the craft."

"Except you weren't to go out of pocket over the thing."

"Kaitlin," he said gently. "I have money. I was a doctor for almost ten years. I have a solid medical pension, plus a military one. I'm not broke."

She began pacing. "Blake's upset."

Ah. Now they were getting somewhere. The boy had taken off in a huff after peppering Dane with questions he wasn't prepared to answer. Okay, he'd been in a crappy mood. Last night the dreams had come again, forcing him to walk the woods before sitting on the boulders with the cold ocean wind whipping spray into his face.

No excuse to take out your cranky mood on Blake. The boy meant no harm. He was curious, like any eleven-year-old. Like Zaakir had been, asking ten thousand questions until Dane would laugh and toss up his hands in mock surrender. *"Enough already! Save some for later."* And he'd tousle the boy's thick, black hair.

How could he tell Kaitlin that her son reminded him

of Zaakir? That every time Dane looked into Blake's dark eyes, he saw Zaakir's? That each visit the boy made to the boathouse had Dane sweating because he knew the kid came looking for a connection of sorts. The way Zaakir, looking for a family, had latched on to Dane.

His days of surrogacy fatherhood were over. He hadn't succeeded with Zaakir and, much as he yearned for the fantasy, he sure as hell wasn't about to practice the family thing with Kaitlin's son. She meant too much for Dane to take that kind of risk, and then leave the kid hanging on an emotional rollercoaster when he packed up and left the island.

Because the day he left Kaitlin's B and B was coming sooner than he anticipated. He decided last night. Once the boat was done, he would be gone.

Kaitlin walked past him to the stencils on the floor that spelled Lady Kaitlin. While he'd been arranging the scripted letters to form the original title, his mind had suddenly conjured *her*—this woman he loved—on his bed in the moonlight. Sensuous, wanton, beautiful… And the words reshaped themselves with a will of their own. *Lady Kaitlin*. Exactly as he saw her that night.

"Why are you changing the name?" she asked.

"It's not how it looks. I was just…" *Fooling around with the letters. Fooling myself into dreaming.* Dreams that included her and the boy and this vessel. Dreams that saw him at the helm, Blake handing out brochures to the tourists on deck as they motored around the inlet during the summer. Dreams that saw Dane mooring the craft at five in the afternoon, then walking up the path for dinner with her and Blake, and spending evenings on the porch….

"Change it back the way it was, Dane. I won't have Blake thinking I'm taking another part of his father away."

Shaun again. "Is that what you think I'm doing?" he asked. "That I'm trying to horn in on the ghost of your husband?"

She blinked. "This has nothing to do with—"

"Doesn't it?" He scraped a hand down his stubbled cheeks. "Look, Kat. I'm not Shaun. I'm just a guy trying to get what's left of his life together. After the other night, I thought you understood that."

She folded her arms against her chest as if holding in her heart. "I love you, Dane. I thought *you* understood that." She stepped closer; he could smell her shampoo, its subtle spice infusing his pillow. She said, "This isn't just about you anymore. This is about all of us."

All of us. As in him, her and Blake. And that was the crux of the matter. He could dream all he wanted, but the truth—the reality—was Kat came with Blake. They were a package, one he either accepted or he didn't.

Round and unwavering, her eyes glued on his. "Your call, Dane," she said softly. "Are you with us or not?"

He took too long thinking, too long tamping back the pressure in his chest.

An edge of her mouth ticked. "Guess that's my answer."

He wanted to call her back, wanted to say, *I'm with you, all the way. I can't do this without you.* In the silence and his loneliness, he clicked on the radio. AC/DC crashed around him, but Kaitlin's words were all he heard.

Chapter Thirteen

Kat got a call from the Burnt Bend Medical Clinic three days later. Could she come to donate blood? The AB supply had reached a low level as a result of a bad traffic accident that morning and while staff had contacted the Seattle blood bank for replenishments, they were also calling their own registry of island residents to donate.

Because the call came at noon and Blake was still too young to stay alone, she took him along to the clinic. She had thought of asking Dane to keep an eye on him, but since their disagreement—if she could call it that—she felt emotionally defeated. He wasn't ready to move forward and until he did, she would continue on as she'd done long before he'd ridden up her driveway that day on his Harley.

Besides, she reminded herself, *you have a child to raise and a business to run. They are your priorities.*

Unfortunately, the mirror told other stories, especially about the sleep she'd lost thinking of Dane, of the emotional morass bogging him down, and the sadness in her heart.

Her eyes exhibited dark circles and her cheeks were more gaunt than usual. And she yawned all day.

Pulling into the clinic's parking lot, she stifled another yawn.

"How long are you gonna be?" Blake whined as they climbed from her car.

"About forty minutes, maybe a little longer. Did you bring your iPod?"

"Yeah. I coulda stayed home, Mom. Next year I'll be twelve and I'll be able to babysit like Becky."

Last year, Addie's eldest daughter had begun watching her siblings and younger cousins.

Kat curved a hand over Blake's shoulder as they walked through the door. *You're growing up way too fast,* she wanted to tell him. *Stay my little boy for a while longer.* But of course she didn't. He would've made a face and mumbled something like, *Oh, Mom, I'm almost taller than you.* As it was, he slipped out from under her hand the second the door closed behind them and headed for the waiting room.

"Stay right there till I get back," she called after him only to receive an over-the-shoulder look that clearly said, *Gimme a break.*

After Kat registered at the reception desk, a nurse—her name tag read Tina—took her down the corridor to an examination room. "Thanks for coming in on such short notice, Mrs. O'Brien," the young woman said.

"Glad to." She got into the recliner set up specifically

for someone giving blood. "I understand there was a traffic accident. Is everyone okay?"

"Yes, thank God. But we want to ensure there's enough of your blood type on hand, regardless."

Kat kept her expression bland. As far as she was concerned, the clinic should keep a healthy store of *every* blood type.

"Did you know you're one of two on Firewood Island who is AB negative?" Tina asked, swabbing the vein inside Kat's elbow before inserting the needle.

"No." What she did know was that a mere one percent of the population had the same rare blood type.

"Well, you're one of our stars." Smiling, the nurse placed several magazines on the small table next to the chair. "I'll be back in five minutes," she said. "Hopefully, with our second star."

Unable to focus on the magazine, Kat's mind whirled around the person who might receive her blood. Man or woman? Her age or Charmaine's? And what if it was a man her mother's age? It didn't mean he was *the closet secret*. He could be…

Someone new to the island.

An octogenarian.

A man of different ethnicity.

"Here we go," Tina said, leading in the other donor and directing him to the opposite recliner.

Kat blinked. Zeb Jantz was AB negative?

"'Morning, Kat," he greeted, settling into the chair as if donning an old comfortable slipper. As if he'd done *this* forever. "Seems we're celebrities today." His bushy brows bunched. He glanced from her face to her arm where the needle extracted a red flow. "You okay?"

"I'm… I'm… Yes." Her thoughts scurried like mice.

"I'm…almost finished." But she couldn't stop staring at the man across the room. Why hadn't she seen it before? Why hadn't she noticed the shape of his nose, a little on the short side—like hers? The way his front teeth had the tiniest gap between them—like hers? And his eyebrows, dark and arched like bows—the way hers were? Though more salt than pepper, his hair was still thick and ruler-straight with a cowlick on the left—a cowlick she saw on Blake every day.

Zeb Jantz…was *he* her father?

"Do I have spaghetti on my shirt or something?" His brown eyes teased.

Flustered he had caught her staring, she turned to her blood bag. "Sorry. I… I was thinking about something, that's all. Tina, I'm done here," she told the nurse. She had to get out of this room and away from the clinic. Away from—from—her *father.* A man who had lived on Firewood Island all *her* life. Who she had spoken to a hundred and one times.

Oh, God. She knew it was him. She just *knew.*

He'd built Charmaine's detached garage, renovated Lee and Rogan's farmhouse, reconstructed Addie's laundry room in her old house… Kat's cabins, her laundry room, her *boat.*

A regular handyman about town.

The moment Tina cleared her, Kat was out of the chair.

"You need to wait fifteen minutes, Ms. O'Brien," she called as Kat hurried from the room.

"I'll drink some juice in the waiting room." Ignoring a wave of light-headedness, she rushed down the hallway.

"Mom?" Blake looked up as her legs gave out and she dropped beside him on the sofa, a little out of breath. "You okay? You don't look so good."

She didn't feel so good either. "Get me some o.j. from the nurse, will you, hon?"

When he did, she held the paper cup with both hands and brought it to her parched lips. So many years she'd wondered, and today she finally knew.

Worry stitched a crease between Blake's eyes. "Should I call Grandma to drive us home?"

An anger Kat hadn't felt in years rose into her throat. Oh, yes, she would see her mother, but not to ask a favor. The one she'd wanted for two decades, the *real* favor, she'd had to discover herself. "I'll be okay in a minute."

"Ms. O'Brien?" Tina stood in front of her with several peeled orange slices on a plastic plate. "It'll help if you eat these."

The lightheadedness began to ebb; she took two slices, popped them into her mouth.

Five minutes later, she breathed the salt-tinged air. "Blake," Kat said as they walked to the old Honda, "do you mind staying at Aunt Addie's for an hour while I get some groceries?" A small lie, but she couldn't confront her mother with her son present.

"I guess," Blake mumbled, clearly not enthused to be hanging out with his female cousins today. Suddenly, he pointed to a blond boy going into the library across the street. "Hey, there's Gerry. Can I go to the library instead?"

Kat noted the boy waving at them. Gerry was Blake's best friend at school. "All right," she said. "But stay at the library until I get back. Do not go anywhere else. Understand?"

"I won't. Thanks, Mom!" Before she could give him further instructions, he dashed to the crosswalk, checked for traffic, then ran to the other side of Main Street. With a wave, he disappeared inside the library.

All right, Mother, Kat mentally told Charmaine. *I hope you're ready because this is one showdown that's been a long time coming.*

Dane carried the sack of groceries around the side of Dalton Foods to the small paved lot at the rear of the store where he had parked the Harley. Tonight he planned to bake a couple of pork chops. Already he was getting tired of eating his own cooking and wished like hell he could invite himself back to Kaitlin's table. *Let's face it, Dane. You wish you could invite yourself back into her life.*

But those days were over. No matter how hard he tried, he couldn't get past this feeling of inadequacy. He couldn't get past believing he'd fail her—and the boy— somehow, someday. Sure, he restored her boat, but that was different. He'd done all the work in private, without her watching, without the boy following like a puppy.

Thinking of Blake, Dane snorted. *You made sure of that, didn't you? Snubbing the kid every time he came around. Scared because you're starting to think of the boy as your own. Like you did before...*

He wondered what Kat would think if she knew the truth.

He should have told her last Friday night.

Dane's chest tightened. He didn't want to think about that night, the one he'd carry in his memories and his heart as long as he lived. The night that had been a gift.

He missed her, missed her smile, her laugh, her voice. Her loving arms, her encouraging words. The faith she had in him. For five days he'd walked in a vacuum, as though someone had hollowed out his heart.

Opening the bike's saddle bags, he wondered if maybe he should see a shrink as his sister suggested.

Suddenly, a piercing whistle erupted from the alley. Then, several gunshots, a harsh cry—all in rapid succession—and Dane dove behind the Harley.

The groceries crashed to the ground. Potatoes rolled around his boots, asparagus thumped under the rear wheel. Crazily, he wondered where the tomatoes had gone. His heart beat like a fist behind his ribs. His breath scraped through his throat. Someone—a kid—was screaming for help.

Haze blurred his eyes. *The fire, the acid! People screaming. Kids crying.* He shook his head. "No-no-no-no!" He was here by the Harley in the parking lot.

Dalton Foods, not Iraq.

He'd had a flashback.

"Mr. Rainhart! Dane! Please—come quick!"

Blake.

Dane sprang to his feet. The boy, panic in his eyes, raced from the alleyway. Deeper into the corridor, several young boys huddled around someone on the ground.

"Gerry's hurt, Dane," Blake yelled. "He needs help!"

Instinct spurred him forward. "What happened?" he asked, sizing up the situation in a glance. Spurts of flame flickered through the kids surrounding the one on the ground.

"These teenagers—" Blake wheezed as he danced on one foot, then the other. "They had a bunch of firecrackers and one—one hit Gerry an' now he's on fire!"

Dane caught Blake's sleeve. "Got your inhaler, son?"

"Yeah, but—"

"Use it. I'll look after Gerry." And then he sprinted down the alley.

At the edge of town, Kat pulled into the driveway of her childhood home and parked beside her mother's

Chevy Malibu. Charmaine seldom locked her door. Still, Kat had always respected her mother's privacy and knocked. Today, however, she walked right in. "Mom? You home?"

No answer. She went through the house, checking the kitchen, the bedrooms, laundry, bathrooms. Returning to the kitchen, she peered out its window. Her mother knelt on a piece of cardboard, pruning the roses bordering a small garden shed. A shed, Kat recalled suddenly, built twenty years ago by Zeb Jantz.

Her father.

With a sigh she stepped out onto the weathered wooden stoop. Would she ever get used to the truth now that it was here?

Charmaine lifted her head. "Goodness, dear. I didn't hear you drive up." She'd set her graying red hair in a thick topknot, and wisps slipped free, clinging to her flushed cheeks. "I was just thinking of you and here you are." Her hands encased in a pair of green rubber gloves, she clipped a long, thorny stem into a rusty bucket. "Is Blake with you?"

"No," Kat said. "Mom, we need to talk. Can you come inside?"

"Sounds serious. Is my grandson okay?"

"He's fine. I'll wait in the kitchen." Kat let the screen slap closed behind her and began pacing the confined area between the cupboards and pantry.

A few minutes later, her mother entered. Watching Kat pace, she toed off her blue clogs and hung her old plaid jacket on a sidebar hook. "What's wrong, Kaitlin Rose?"

Kaitlin Rose. Charmaine never called Kat by her full name unless she was angry—or worried. Extremely worried. Looking at her mother's bleached complexion, Kat suspected the latter.

"Thirty-four years," she said, halting her frenetic pace. She crossed her arms against her wild heart. "And finally I know."

If possible, Charmaine's face whitened even more. She went to a chair, pulled it out and sank down. "How?"

So. Her mother understood the reason for Kat's visit. She pulled in a hard breath. "The accident this morning."

Charmaine's head snapped up. She seemed to age on the spot. "What accident?"

Kat explained about the two-car crash on the other side of the island, and the medical clinic's call for type AB negative blood.

"Who was hurt?" Charmaine's eyes beseeched Kat's.

"Not him."

The wash of relief in her mother's face was palpable. Placing her palms against her cheeks, she bowed her head. "So Zeb was called as a donor," she whispered.

"Yes." Kat watched her mother set trembling hands in her lap. She would not feel sorry. She would not. She wanted to rush across the room and wrap Charmaine in her arms and cry on her shoulder the way she had when she was four and scraped a knee.

Kat paced again. "I hate that you hid this from me for so many years, Mom. It was wrong, so damned wrong."

"I should've told you," Charmaine whispered. "I don't know why I didn't. I was so scared."

Arms hugging her middle, Kat stared at her mother from across the room. "Who was he to you?"

"The love of my life."

"Excuse me?"

Charmaine closed her eyes. "Oh, Kat. I've loved

Zeb Jantz all my life. We grew up together and were best friends."

"Then why didn't you marry him?"

"Because… He joined the seminary. His parents wanted him to be a priest. You see, he came from a large Catholic family, and was the oldest son. For generations one male always became a priest."

"And he didn't have the guts to stand up to them?"

"You don't understand. Ours was a very different generation than yours or even Blake's. Things are less…traditional now."

"So you married Lee's dad instead."

"I was defiant. I wanted to hurt Zeb, so I married the first man who asked, but fool is me. Zeb tried the seminary, and hated every minute. Two years later, he quit. By the time he came back to the island, I was in the throes of divorce from Lee's dad."

"So why didn't you marry Zeb then?"

Charmaine looked at Kat with bleak eyes. "He'd married someone else before he returned." Her smile held a universe of sadness. "Seems he had a streak of defiance as well."

"Did he marry before or after…?" *Me*.

"Before."

"Are you saying you had—had—"

"Sex with a married man? Yes, Kaitlin, I did. And I'm not proud of that, but *you*…" Her mother's eyes were full of emotion. "Oh, honey, I'm so very proud you are my daughter. You and Blake have made my life complete."

Words seemed to vanish from Kat's tongue. She stared at Charmaine in disbelief. All through their teenage years, Charmaine had preached to Kat, Lee and Addie about abstaining from premarital sex and, if it did happen, to always practice safety to avoid pregnancy. And then Addie got pregnant and Charmaine, along with Addie's father, convinced their daughter to give up her child.

Yet, years before, Charmaine had *not* given up Kat.

"Say something," the older woman whispered.

Kat clung to the counter. "I'm dumbfounded."

Charmaine touched her forehead with shaky fingers. "I know you're thinking about Addie."

"And then some."

"As I said, I've made some huge mistakes in my life, Kaitlin, but you were never one. *Never.*"

"Does Zeb know?"

"Yes. He suspected it for a long time. He asked once, but I wouldn't answer him." Charmaine gazed out the kitchen window where, in a cloudless sky, the March sun warmed the backyard. "Which, I suppose was an answer in itself. It wasn't hard to see, though. You always looked more like him than me."

"Did you ever tell him?" Zeb and his wife had been childless. The fact he suspected he had a daughter living practically next door, but couldn't claim her, must have tormented him.

"After Ruth died five years ago of pancreatic cancer."

"He's known *that* long and never said a thing?" Something in Kat withered.

"I forbade it."

Of course. Kat could imagine Charmaine laying down the law on her closet skeleton. Well, enough was enough. Jaw rigid, she said, "Blake has a right to know his grandfather." She would not keep secrets from her son. She would do what Yolanda Rainhart had done for *her* son: instill integrity and honor by example.

A tear slipped down Charmaine's cheek. "You're a good mother, Kat. Far better than I've been. Zeb will be over the moon. He's been waiting for this day for a long, long time."

That surprised Kat. "You're not going to talk me out of it?"

For the first time, her mother smiled. "No, dear. This is your life now, not mine."

Amazing how light with relief she felt. Easing her fingers from the counter's edge, Kat pulled in a long breath. "Thank you."

Charmaine came out of the chair and went to her daughter. Her arms wrapped Kat in a tight hug. "It's me who needs to thank you," she whispered. "I love you, Kaitlin. You and your sisters and my grandbabies are my world. Will you ever forgive me?"

Kat hesitated. She could continue to let her anger fester or she could forgive her mother. She pressed her cheek against Charmaine's. "I love you, too. And there's nothing to forgive. No one's perfect, Mom." She thought of the years she'd complained to Shaun and her sister—even to Dane—about Charmaine. Finally, she drew back. "I need to go. Blake's waiting for me at the library."

Charmaine took a container of blueberry muffins from the refrigerator. "Made these fresh this morning."

Kat smiled. "I will admit you're a terrific grand-mother. But don't let it go to your head."

Charmaine chuckled. "Noted."

They walked to the front door. On the threshold, Kat said, "By the way, Addie, Lee and I all know Zeb's interested in you."

Charmaine blinked. "Is that so?"

Kat looked into her mother's eyes. "He's a good man and you've waited long enough. Go for it."

With a wink, she left Charmaine sputtering on the stoop.

* * *

Carrying Gerry in his arms, Dane rushed through the electronic doors of Burnt Bend's Medical Clinic. "Flash fire burn," he told the triage nurse at the ER desk. "Second degree. Left ankle and shin."

"Down here." The woman came around the counter and led Dane to the first gurney in the hallway.

"Is he gonna be all right?" Blake asked at Dane's elbow as he laid Gerry on the stretcher. Face pale, the boy moaned through clenched teeth.

"He'll be fine," Dane replied. "Got any allergies, Gerry?"

The boy's head waggled on the paper pillow. "Nuhhh."

Dane took Gerry's wrist and counted off the seconds on his watch before telling the nurse, "Pulse ninety-eight. We need a saline IV. Don't want him dehydrating."

"Are you a doctor?"

"Yes, Dane Rainhart. I was a trauma surgeon in Iraq."

Blake's jaw dropped as the woman disappeared into a room across the hall. Ten seconds later, Dane's father, in a pristine white lab coat, came through the door. Their eyes met briefly before Ben Rainhart went to the boy on the stretcher.

Watching his father's gentle hands examine the wounds, something in Dane shifted, quieted. "He got in the way of a firecracker behind Dalton Foods," he said, because Ben would want to know. "Teenagers fooling around." He offered Kat's dark-eyed son a quick smile. "Blake here called for help."

"And you went," Ben said gruffly.

Dane shrugged. He'd doused the flames with his jacket before slicing several scraps of denim from the boy's skin. Still, blisters quilted the ankle. On the shin, however, some had broken and acted as glue with the fabric; he had left those patches for the medical team.

"My mom and dad," Gerry rasped. "They're gonna be so disappointed."

"No, son, they won't," Ben said gently. "This was an accident."

"But I shouldna left the house. I was supposed to sweep the garage and take out the trash. But then I... I left." Gerry's mouth twisted; his eyes glimmered.

Dane patted the boy's arm. "I'll explain everything to them, Gerry. You just get better, all right?"

Dane watched the nurse roll her patient down the hall. He turned to Blake. "Where's your mom?"

The boy's eyes rounded. "Oh, man! I was supposed to meet her at the library." Checking his Iron Man wristwatch, he groaned. "Like fifteen minutes ago."

"We'll find her. She got a cell phone?"

"Dane," Ben said. Emotion glowed behind the senior Rainhart's wire-rimmed glasses. "I'm damned proud of you."

Dane experienced a streak of pleasure. Yeah, *he'd* turned a corner—and, God, it felt good.

With a nod to his father, he strode down the hallway. By the time he was through the emergency doors, his big, crazy-assed grin threatened to hurt his face. He needed to find Kat, needed to tell her about this—this goofy lightness he felt, this freedom. Freedom from a long winter in solitary confinement. Hell, if he wasn't careful, he'd start kicking up his heels like one of those actors on *Dancing With The Stars*.

He flipped his cell phone open and called the number Blake had given. She answered on the fourth ring.

"Kat," he said, heading for the sidewalk along Main. "Blake's with me at the medical clinic."

"Omigod! I've been looking all over for him. What happened? Is he okay?"

"He's fine, his friend had an accident. We just dropped him off at the E.R. Where are you?"

"At Coffee Sense. I thought maybe he'd come here for a hot chocolate. Oh! There you are. I see you."

Dane looked toward the cove and its horseshoe boardwalk, and there she was, waving at him as she approached the only light-controlled intersection in town. A jolt of happiness slammed into him. Her dark hair swung like a short silky veil along her jaw. Today she wore black slacks and a harvest-gold jacket zipped halfway to reveal a green sweater beneath. He could hear the *pit-put* of her spiked boot heels as she drew closer. For two beats, her brown eyes clung to Dane's before flicking to Blake. A small frown replaced her grin.

"You are so in trouble, mister," she said to her son, though worry rather than anger inflected her voice. "What did I tell you about staying in one place?"

"Sorry, Mom."

"Never mind. We'll deal with that later. What happened to Gerry?"

"We couldn't find any books we wanted to read in the library so we went outside for a minute and then… We saw these guys with firecrackers and then after Gerry got burned and Dane carried him to the clinic and—and—Mom, you should see his leg! It's like gross, but Dane knew what to do and—"

"Stop." She held up ten fingers. "Slow down and start from the beginning. I want all the details."

Dane had to hide a grin. She was one beautiful

woman when her mothering instincts flared. Suddenly an image of her heavy with his child flashed into his mind. Was it possible? Would she even want another child, *his* child? Looking at her avid brown eyes, hearing her voice… Hell, why *couldn't* they begin again? The three of them together?

"Right, Dane?" The boy tugged his sleeve hauling him back to the moment at hand. "You saved Gerry from getting third degree burns, didn't you?"

"Nope," he replied. "You did."

"Me?"

Dane peeked over at Kat. "Yep," he said with a wink in her direction. "You're the one who ran for help when all the other kids did nothing. It was you, Blake. You saved Gerry from a very bad burn."

"Really?" The boy grew an inch with Dane's praise.

Kat looked from one to the other. Her frown vanished and something he hadn't dared imagine—pride—glowed in her face. "Seems the two of you had quite a day."

"A good day," Dane supplied. *A new day.*

Comprehension brimmed in her dark eyes. "Well. I think that calls for some apple crumble a la mode. My treat. What do you say, guys?"

Dane flashed Blake a grin. "I say your mom's got a deal, wouldn't you, buddy?"

"Does this mean I won't be grounded?" the boy asked.

Kat laughed. "Don't get your hopes up, pal."

Dane's heart lifted higher. Yes, a damn good day.

Chapter Fourteen

Something had changed. Kat felt it the instant Dane's eyes locked on her and he took her hand, and the three of them set off for the coffee shop on Burnt Bend's wharf. She felt it while they ate their crumble cakes and rehashed the past hour, and Blake sent Dane glances of adoration. There was no doubt that today he and Dane had discovered some kind of bond, and Dane had come to a decision, one he was eager to explain to Kat privately. She, too, wanted to tell him about her meeting with Charmaine.

They laughed and smiled and talked until thirty minutes later, she said, "Time for us to go home, son."

"Aww…" he moaned.

"Listen to your mom, bud." Dane tousled her son's hair, a gesture that usually had her son jerking away with a scowl.

Not today. Today, the tousling resulted in a sheepish grin.

Back at the street intersection, Kat took heart in the moment. "Will we see you for dinner tonight?" she asked Dane.

He looked at Blake. "Okay if I come, tiger? I'd hate to miss your mom's cooking."

"Sure! And afterward we can play Rock Band. You can be lead singer."

Back and forth they chatted and chuckled, and Kat's heart felt full as they walked toward Dalton Foods. Their vehicles were behind the store in the parking lot, but she needed some fruits and vegetables for tonight's meal. Mentally debating her selection, she suddenly faltered in her pace.

"Kat?" Dane asked, setting a hand on her arm.

At the curb twenty feet away, Zeb Jantz loaded two large bags of dog food into his pickup.

At their approach, his head turned. His gaze swooped over Dane and Blake, then settled on her.

"Kat."

"Zeb." *I know who you are!* she wanted to shout. Instead, she pressed her lips to seal her knowledge. This was the man who'd respected her mother enough to keep her secret. Her peripheral vision caught Dane's scrutiny; still she couldn't tear her gaze from the older man. Slowly, slowly his smile faded. Unable to bear it a second longer, she blurted, "I know. I...*know*."

Five long seconds passed before his face relaxed and his brown eyes, so like hers, lit. "I'm glad, Kat."

Gripping Dane's hand, she walked toward her father. "Let's have coffee one day soon. Maybe catch up." *Thirty-four years worth.*

Against his brown, weathered face, his teeth flashed in a grin, and again she recognized familiarity. "I'd like that." Turning to Blake, he said, "Take care of your mom, son. She donated blood today."

"Yes, sir, I will."

With a nod to Dane, the older man got into his pickup and drove away. Kat stared after him. "Never in a million years did I think this day would come."

"Why, Mom?" Blake asked. "What's so special about today?"

"Everything." She laughed. "Just…everything."

"Great. Can we go now?"

"In a few minutes. First, I need some groceries for tonight. Want to grab a cart and find some apples and bananas?"

"Twinkies, too?"

"Oh, heck, why not?" When he'd vanished into the store, she said to Dane, "Meet you back home?"

"I'll be there." His eyes were the color of the cove's water. "And Kat? Your father's a good man."

She released a soft laugh. Of course he'd guess. "He is, isn't he?"

Heedless that they stood on a public sidewalk, Dane touched his mouth to hers. "I love you." And then he was striding around the corner of the building and out of sight.

Kat swiped a tear off her cheek. If she lived to a hundred and ten, she'd remember this day forever, this bright, warm day with its promise and hope.

Dane sat on Kaitlin's living room sofa, sipping the decaf coffee she'd brought on a tray. He had wanted to stay in the kitchen, laden with the aroma of her cooking and freshly baked molasses cookies.

He loved her kitchen. He loved the way she moved around the big, green worktable. He loved the peace he felt there—even when she slipped from the room. The walls brimmed with the essence that was his Kat.

His Kat. When had he begun thinking of her as his? *The moment she brought you those tulips.*

His chest rumbled with a chuckle. In truth, he would've given his right arm to be *hers* in that moment.

What's so funny?" she asked, edging her toes under his thigh from where she sat in the opposite corner of the couch. Tonight she'd clipped a wing of her glossy hair behind one ear. He let his eyes linger on hers, then dip to the slenderness of her neck, and down to the green sweater shaping her breasts. More than anything, he wanted to lean over and set his hands there. To taste her skin, to know again the flavor of her warmth, softness, wetness—

He looked away.

"Dane?"

"I was just thinking about the day you showed me how to care for your tulips. They lasted more than a week, by the way."

"That's good. Help yourself to anything from my garden."

This time he laughed aloud. "Oh, honey. You can bet I will." He couldn't resist. Setting aside his mug of coffee, he slid across the couch and kissed her. "Hmm," he said when he was done. "Best tasting *two* lips I've known."

Grinning, she caught his chin, studied his mouth. "I agree." Then her gaze lifted and her grin fled. "You changed my life, Dane."

"Me, too." He traced the contour of her eyebrows. "Kat, my father's asked me to meet with a Seattle surgeon looking for a consultant to help people with disabilities—in particular veterans suffering from PTSD. Because of my experience, he feels I might be able to talk them through whatever procedures they need." Easing back, Dane pulled her with him to cuddle in the corner of the couch. "There's one problem. It would mean leaving the island."

She toyed with the brown cotton cuff of his polo shirt. "What do *you* want?"

He shrugged. "On the one hand, it would allow me back into medicine, on the other…" He set his mouth against her hair. "You and Blake are here."

Her fingers hesitated and he felt as though he toed the edge of a precipice. "Yes," she said. "We are. Except, this is your life, not ours."

"No," he said. "Ours *together*. You and I and Blake could—"

"Stop." She pushed off the sofa. "I won't be your deciding factor, Dane."

He rose. "Kat, I've already—"

"I think you should go."

Smiling sadly, she glanced toward the front door. He got the message. The evening was finished. Their great day with all its amazing surprises was finished. *They* were finished. But she'd gotten it wrong, all wrong.

He watched her walk back to her kitchen, black skirt swinging prettily around her knees. *Fine, then,* he thought. *We'll see what you say tomorrow.*

Shoving his hands into his trouser pockets, he headed for the door. Ten minutes later, metal music belted from the boathouse radio.

Blake crept back upstairs to his bedroom. He'd come down to the kitchen for a glass of milk and heard Dane telling Mom he was getting a job in Seattle. Blake didn't really understand why, but he didn't want Dane moving away from Burnt Bend. Well, he sorta knew why. He liked the guy. He'd always liked him, even when he was complaining to Gerry.

Dane was cool. He could rebuild motorcycles and boats, and he was a doctor. He'd helped Blake when he hurt his leg and then today he'd rushed Gerry to the Medical Clinic.

But it wasn't just that. Dane was a good dude—and Blake had to admit—the guy liked Mom and she liked him. All you had to do was see the way they looked at each other.

But tonight Mom had sounded so sad when she heard about the Seattle job, almost like she wanted to cry. Blake didn't want his mom crying anymore. She'd cried so much when his dad died.

Flopping on his bed, he reached for the phone on his night table. Gerry would know what to do.

"Hey," he said when his friend answered. "How ya feeling?"

"Okay. Leg still hurts some, but Dr. Rainhart said that'll go away soon."

"Dane's a doctor, too, y'know."

"Yeah," Gerry said. "The nurse told me. Think he'll start working at the clinic, now?"

Blake's chest felt funny, like a rock sat there. "He's leaving."

"Leaving? Where to?"

Blake explained what he'd heard.

"Oh, man, that sucks. Sorry, I meant, that's good. Right? 'Specially with him hanging around your mom an' all."

Blake cringed. He shouldn't have told Gerry all those mean things about Dane. "No, it's not good. It's making Mom sad." He picked a thumbnail. "Ger, I gotta ask… Is your stepdad nice sometimes?"

"Yeah, dude, he is. I know I complain about the way he acts when I don't do chores or homework, and talk back to Mom and stuff. But…I dunno. He's like the dad I never had. He was crazy worried when him and Mom came to the clinic. And he kept wiping her tears. He really loves her, y'know?"

The pressure lifted from Blake's chest. "Yeah," he said, thinking of his mom. "I know."

The next morning, Kat sat staring into her coffee while her son, dressed in his pjs and wrapped in his bed quilt, hunched over a bowl of cereal. He'd woken grumpy and irritable and at the moment pushed his spoon around his shredded wheat rather than eating it.

"What's the matter, son?" Kat asked. He'd never been robust, but this morning his freckles stood out more than usual against his complexion. She felt his forehead. A little warm, but nothing unusual considering he'd climbed from bed five minutes before.

"Can I watch TV?" he asked, pushing away the bowl. "I'm not very hungry."

Kat didn't have the heart to argue. Normally, she'd never allow TV at eight-thirty in the morning, but today was different. Today, she'd risen to sit in the old walnut rocking chair in her bedroom, watching the dawn peel back the night layer by layer while her mind, full of Dane, whirled with a thousand words, a thousand scenarios.

He would be leaving soon. Leaving the island— and her. Silly, foolish her. Yesterday, in Burnt Bend,

she believed they had come to some kind of tele-
pathic decision, one that needed no words, only those
in their hearts.

But then last night he'd told her of his father's con-
nections and she'd realized her own misconstrued as-
sumptions. The good day he'd alluded to meant he was
ready to get back to the world of medicine, a world
beyond this little island.

And yet he'd kissed her before dinner last night…
Kissed like a man in love. How, then, could he leave?

"Mom?" Blake still waited permission for the TV. "Is
Dane leaving?"

Kat's hand jerked on her coffee mug. Had he over-
heard them talking last night? "His registration with us
is for only three months, Blake." *Not forever.* "And if the
boat's finished before then, it's possible he'll cut his
stay short." Best to say it aloud and prepare him as well
as herself.

"Where will he go?"

"I don't know."

He burrowed deeper into his quilt. "I'm gonna watch
TV."

When he'd shuffled off, comforter dragging on his
heels, she rose to attend to the breakfast dishes and
start her day.

Soapy water filled the sink, when a thumping
sounded on the back door.

"Kaitlin, open up," a man's voice called.

Adrenaline shooting down her spine, Kat hurried
into the mudroom. He never hammered on the door.
Something's wrong, was her only thought as she swung
open the door.

And there he stood, grinning down at her, blue eyes

sparkling with excitement, gold hair mused from the sea-scented breeze—a James Dean rebel-without-a-cause facsimile in a black fisherman's sweater, jeans, and sturdy boots, his thumbs hooked in his hip pockets.

"'Morning, Kat." He bent and kissed her swiftly on the mouth. "Blake up yet?"

Two seconds. She swallowed, told her heart to calm, her insides not to dissolve. "He is, but—"

"What's going on, Mom?" her son called from the kitchen.

"Rise and shine, buddy." Dane glanced over her shoulder. "Got something to show you both."

"Is it cool?" the boy asked eagerly, fairly dancing on his toes.

"Oh, yeah. So, hurry and get dressed, okay?"

"'Kay!" He shot away.

Amazed at her son's transformation from despondent to enthusiastic, Kat stared after Blake. "Well," she said with a half-laugh. "Seems you've got a fan."

An emotion that had her heart singing filled Dane's eyes. He stepped inside and closed the door. Then he took her in his arms.

"Kat," he whispered against her hair. Warm and mobile and tasting faintly of mint, his mouth found hers and all her worries vanished. Drifting on sensation and heat, she wrapped her arms around his neck and hung on.

She lost track of seconds, minutes, until her son's feet thundered down the stairs. Dane snatched Kat's pink jacket off the hook and held it for her to slip into. "It's a cool morning," he said, his freshly shaven jaw ruddy under his tanned skin.

Kat wondered if her own cheeks were flushed.

"Where we going?" Dressed in jeans and a sweatshirt, Blake plopped onto the floor to drag on his sneakers.

Dane winked at Kat, and her heart rate leveled. "You'll see."

He opened the door and they stepped into the crisp morning air bearing the musk of loamy earth and sea brine. Taking the lead, he walked around the house and headed down the path through the trees to the boathouse. There, he rolled back the big doors before ushering them inside.

"The *Kat Lady,*" he said, pride in his voice. "All ready and set to go."

"Wow." Blake stared in awe. Walking toward the bow, his dark eyes brimmed with admiration at the intricately restored hull. "When'd you finish?"

"Well…" Dane rubbed the back of his neck, and offered a crooked grin that had Kat wanting to grab his face and kiss him into next year. "I stayed up until four this morning."

"You did?" she and Blake said in unison.

"Guess I overdid it, huh?"

Blake touched the silken wood. "No way. She's *beautiful.*"

"I couldn't agree more, buddy. She's the most beautiful lady you'll ever see." Except, Dane wasn't looking at the trawler. He was looking straight at Kat. "You won't find another like her."

Blake continued to study the finish, the sleek modern propeller. "Where'd you learn all this stuff about boats?"

"My grandfather."

"Man, he sure knew what he was doing. Can I go up on deck?"

Dane glanced at Kat. "Ask your mom. She's the captain."

"Can I, Mom?"

Kat nodded and pushed a fist against her prickling nose.

Blake's brows pleated. "Aw, jeez... You gonna cry?"

"I th-think so," she mumbled and then Dane was pulling her into his arms, and she didn't care that her son stood beside them.

Her world was no longer the same, and it felt good and bad at the same time. She buried her face against the softness of Dane's sweater and attempted to bite back the swell in her chest and throat, but the surge was too powerful. The boat was finished. His reason for staying had ended, just as her reason for keeping the boat had ended. It was time to take that step forward, sell the vessel—and let Dane go to wherever he needed to go. Yesterday, she had witnessed his transformation at the clinic, heard his decision last night in her house. These past weeks, repairing the *Kat Lady* had healed him, emotionally, spiritually, and he was ready to adapt to the changes in his life. She should be too.

But, oh, God, it was hard. She thought she was done hurting after Shaun's death, but this... This was almost as bad, because Dane would be somewhere in the world, somewhere out there, and she'd be here on the island. Without him.

"Kat," he murmured against her hair. "Why the tears? I thought you'd be happy."

"I am, but..."

"Is it because of the changes I made?"

"Nooo—" She hiccupped, unable to stop the tears.

"Mom." Voice ripe with worry, Blake tugged at her arm. "What's wrong?"

She shook her head, smearing tears across Dane's chest. *Get a grip, Kat. You're making a fool of yourself.*

Easing away, she palmed her cheeks, tried to smile, to laugh, except the sound was blubbery in her ears. "I don't know what got into me."

Dane hadn't released her left elbow. His eyes coaxed, *Tell me.*

"I'm okay," she said, sniffing loudly. "The boat's lovely, Dane. I can't praise your work enough."

"I don't want praise, Kat." Curling his fingers around hers, he brought their hands against his chest. "What I want is to put the *Kat Lady* on the water, operate her as a tour boat. What do you say, Blake?" he asked without looking at her son. "Want to be first mate on weekends and during the summer months?"

"Yeah!" The boy bounced on the balls of his feet. "Oh, man—can I, Mom, can I?"

"But…" Kat clamped her bottom lip and looked at Dane. "I thought you were going to Seattle as a medical consultant."

He gave her a lazy smile. "Honey, I tried to tell you last night that I told Dad I'd rather do consulting with him—here—during the winter months." His brow furrowed. "Unless you had other plans?"

"Other plans?"

He glanced at the craft in her cradle. "Sell—"

"No, Mom!" Blake interjected. "Don't sell. *Pleeease.* Dane and I can run her. Please, Mom."

Kat let out a watery laugh and this time it felt good. "All right. We can try it."

"Not try," Dane said. "Do it."

"Do it," she repeated and her heart warmed at the look in his eyes.

"Blake," Dane said. "There's only one job left. I need you to repaint the boat's name. The stencils are all up on the wood, so once I rig the scaffolding you can pick the color you want."

Blake ran around to the stern of the boat where the name had once blazed out in red lettering. "I thought you were changing her name to *Lady Kaitlin*," he called.

"Nope." Dane smiled at Kat. "I think we should keep the name your dad chose."

On the other side of the shed, silence fell.

Dane whispered, "Do you have any idea how much I love you?" His eyes were dark and full of emotion. He wanted to kiss her, and she wanted to kiss him back.

Behind them, a scuffle. "Oh, man." Blake grimaced in typical eleven-year-old fashion. "Are you guys gonna kiss?"

Kat smiled but didn't move from the arms of the man she loved. "Would that bother you, son?"

"Guess not if he's your boyfriend."

"Would you mind if he was?" she asked.

"Uh-uh. It'd be sorta cool."

Kat laughed. "Really?"

"Uh-huh. Can I go call Gerry and tell him about the *Kat Lady?*"

"Absolutely," Kat said.

Blake rushed to the doors, and stopped. "Mom? Can we get a new photo album for the pictures?"

"Pictures?"

"You know…the ones with me and Dane operating the *Kat Lady?*"

Kat looked at her son. "You bet," she said softly.

"Awesome."

Alone at last, she threaded her fingers through Dane's hair, loving the texture, the warmth. The shape of him against her body. "*Are* you my boyfriend?" she teased.

His blue eyes darkened. "I'd rather be your husband, Kat. I'd like to be the guy Blake can count on when he needs a man's help. I want to share a home with you and him, maybe give him a little brother or sister." Throat working a swallow, he rasped, "I know this is soon, but will you marry me, my Lady Kaitlin?"

"Yes," she whispered, her vision blurring again. "Oh, yes."

Epilogue

The May Memorial Day weekend saw Kat standing on the boathouse pier with Dane, Blake and a dozen of their extended family. They'd all come to celebrate the *Kat Lady*'s initiation day. For the first time in four years the vessel bobbed gently on dockside waters. With the help of Kat's brothers-in-law, Skip and Rogan, and her father Zeb, Dane had launched the boat yesterday in preparation for this moment.

Kat's hair tossed in the ocean breeze and her eyes stung with its bite, yet she couldn't stop grinning at Dane. Today marked the beginning of the rest of their lives as a couple.

How she wanted to tell him of the joy in her heart. That she loved him more each day and, if she lived to be a very old woman, she still wouldn't be able to describe the depth of her emotion. And she knew it was the same for him. They had spoken often of their feelings since that evening he'd walked out of her house to finish the boat's renovations. Since that morning he'd asked her to marry him.

They would exchange vows in a simple ceremony on the *Kat Lady* the last Saturday in September. The date had been Blake's idea. "*It's right after my birthday,*" he'd told Kat and Dane. "*We can have a two-day party!*"

"*Well,*" Dane had drawled with a wink at Kat. "*Who can argue that?*"

Now, tucking Kat under his arm, protective against the wind's nip, he bent to her ear. "Ready?"

"I've been ready since you stood in the carport, dripping with rain."

They exchanged smiles.

"All set, sailor?" Dane called to Blake, who was rushing from aunt to uncle to cousin with leaflets highlighting the Country Cabin on the Sea charter schedules and services.

"Yup!" The boy shoved the last copies into his grandmother's hand. "Make sure everyone gets one, Grams," he said before dashing up the short gangplank ahead of Kat and Dane.

The moment had come. The boat would do its first run around Firewood Island as a touring vessel. Kat laughed as Blake, wearing a similar orange preserver to hers and Dane's, rushed to unfurl the new American flag at the stern. A minute later, he flipped the switch and brought up the anchor.

"*Kat Lady* is a go," he yelled.

On a two-fingered salute, Dane disappeared into the pilothouse.

Addie and Skip, Lee and Rogan—along with their

children—waved from the pier. Kat's gaze softened when she saw Zeb with his arm around her mother. Kat blew them a kiss, which her father pretended to catch and lay against Charmaine's cheek. "Love you both," Kat mouthed.

Bliss shone in their eyes.

As Dane turned on the engines and edged from the wharf, a cheer rose from the well-wishers. "Bye! Bon voyage! See you in two hours!"

The boat chugged toward the dazzling waters of Admiralty Inlet.

"Do you think Dane will let me steer the boat, Mom?" Blake asked, his cheeks ruddy from the crisp air.

"Let's go see."

In the pilothouse, Dane sat behind the big, wooden wheel. As always, when it was only Blake and Kat, his hands were bare. She knew the day would soon come when he'd feel safe among their families without the gloves.

"Hey, buddy." He canted a grin over his shoulder that made Kat's legs watery, and Blake beam. "Ready to steer for a while?" As her son climbed into the captain's chair, Dane picked up a camera Kat hadn't noticed before. "First," he said, snapping several shots of a grinning Blake, "something for that new album."

After they had discussed how to read the instrument panel, Dane told Blake to "keep it steady" while he took some photos of Kat on deck.

Outside, the sun scattered diamonds across the wavelets, while behind the boat five seagulls winged the ocean breeze.

Dane pulled Kat into his arms. "Happy?"

"Beyond words."

"Same," he whispered, and bent to kiss her tenderly before she nestled back against his chest.

A frothy wake trailed the waters from boat to pier and, above, cirrus clouds sketched the sky, ocean to island. *Little roads leading home,* Kat thought.

She burrowed deeper into Dane's arms.

They were home at last.

* * * * *

*In honor of our 60th anniversary,
Harlequin® American Romance® is celebrating
by featuring an all-American male each month,
all year long with*
MEN MADE IN AMERICA!
*This June, we'll be featuring American men
living in the West.*

Here's a sneak preview of
THE CHIEF RANGER *by Rebecca Winters.*

*Chief Ranger Vance Rossiter has to confront the sister
of a man who died while under Vance's watch…
and also confront his attraction to her.*

"Chief Ranger Rossiter?" The sight of the woman who'd stepped inside Vance's office brought him to his feet. "I'm Rachel Darrow. Your secretary said I should come right in."

"Please," he said, walking around his desk to shake her hand. At a glance he estimated she was in her mid-twenties. Her feminine curves did wonders for the pale blue T-shirt and jeans she was wearing. "Ranger Jarvis informed me there's a young boy with you."

The unfriendly expression in her beautiful green eyes caught him off guard. "Yes," was her clipped reply. "When we arrived in Yosemite the ranger told me I couldn't go anywhere in the park until I talked to you first."

"That's right."

"Knowing you wanted this meeting to be private, he offered to show my nephew around Headquarters."

So this woman was the victim's sister…. "What's his name?"

"Nicky."

The boy who haunted Vance's dreams now had a name. "How old is he?"

"He turned six three weeks ago. Were you the man in charge when my brother and sister-in-law were killed?"

"Yes. To tell you I'm sorry for what happened couldn't begin to convey my feelings."

The woman's gaze didn't flicker. "I won't even try to describe mine. Just tell me one thing. Was their accident preventable?"

"Yes," he answered without hesitation.

"In other words, the people working under you fell asleep on your watch and two lives were snuffed out as a result."

Hearing it put like that, he had to set the record straight. "My staff had nothing to do with it. I, myself, could have prevented the loss of life."

Ms. Darrow's expression hardened. "So you admit culpability."

"Yes. I take full blame."

A look of pain crossed over her features. "You can just stand there and admit it?" Her cry echoed that of his own tortured soul.

"Yes." He sucked in his breath.

"I work for a cruise line. Aboard ship, it's the captain's responsibility to maintain rigid safety regulations. If a disaster like that had happened while he was in charge he would have been relieved of his command and never given another ship again."

Rachel Darrow couldn't know she was preaching to the converted. "If you've come to the park with the intention of bringing a lawsuit against me for negligence, maybe you should." It would only be what he deserved.

"Maybe I will."

In the next instant, she wheeled around and hurried out of his office. Vance could have gone after her, but it would cause a scene, something he was loath to do for a variety of reasons. In the first place, he needed to cool down before he approached her again.

The discovery of the Darrows' frozen bodies had affected every ranger in the park. A little boy had been orphaned—a boy whose aunt was all he had left.

* * * * *

*Will Rachel allow Vance to explain—
and will she let him into her heart?
Find out in
THE CHIEF RANGER
Available June 2009 from
Harlequin® American Romance®.*

We'll be spotlighting a different series every month
throughout 2009 to celebrate our 60th anniversary.

Look for Harlequin®
American Romance® in June!

Join us for a year-long celebration of the rugged
American male! From cops to cowboys—
Men Made in America has the hero
you've been dreaming about!

Look for

The Chief Ranger

by Rebecca Winters, on sale in June!

Bachelor CEO by Michele Dunaway	July
The Rodeo Rider by Roxann Delaney	August
Doctor Daddy by Jacqueline Diamond	September

You're invited to join our Tell Harlequin Reader Panel!

By joining our new reader panel you will:

- Receive Harlequin® books—they are FREE and yours to keep with no obligation to purchase anything!
- Participate in fun online surveys
- Exchange opinions and ideas with women just like you
- Have a say in our new book ideas and help us publish the best in women's fiction

In addition, you will have a chance to win great prizes and receive special gifts!
See Web site for details. Some conditions apply.
Space is limited.

To join, visit us at
www.TellHarlequin.com.

REQUEST YOUR FREE BOOKS!
2 FREE NOVELS PLUS 2 FREE GIFTS!

SPECIAL EDITION®
Life, Love and Family!

YES! Please send me 2 FREE Silhouette Special Edition® novels and my 2 FREE gifts (gifts are worth about $10). After receiving them, if I don't wish to receive any more books, I can return the shipping statement marked "cancel." If I don't cancel, I will receive 6 brand-new novels every month and be billed just $4.24 per book in the U.S. or $4.99 per book in Canada. That's a savings of at least 15% off the cover price! It's quite a bargain! Shipping and handling is just 50¢ per book.* I understand that accepting the 2 free books and gifts places me under no obligation to buy anything. I can always return a shipment and cancel at any time. Even if I never buy another book from Silhouette, the two free books and gifts are mine to keep forever.

235 SDN EYN4 335 SDN EYPG

Name	(PLEASE PRINT)	
Address		Apt. #
City	State/Prov.	Zip/Postal Code

Signature (if under 18, a parent or guardian must sign)

Mail to the Silhouette Reader Service:
IN U.S.A.: P.O. Box 1867, Buffalo, NY 14240-1867
IN CANADA: P.O. Box 609, Fort Erie, Ontario L2A 5X3

Not valid to current subscribers of Silhouette Special Edition books.

Want to try two free books from another line?
Call 1-800-873-8635 or visit www.morefreebooks.com.

* Terms and prices subject to change without notice. Prices do not include applicable taxes. Sales tax applicable in N.Y. Canadian residents will be charged applicable provincial taxes and GST. Offer not valid in Quebec. This offer is limited to one order per household. All orders subject to approval. Credit or debit balances in a customer's account(s) may be offset by any other outstanding balance owed by or to the customer. Please allow 4 to 6 weeks for delivery. Offer available while quantities last.

Your Privacy: Silhouette is committed to protecting your privacy. Our Privacy Policy is available online at www.eHarlequin.com or upon request from the Reader Service. From time to time we make our lists of customers available to reputable third parties who may have a product or service of interest to you. If you would prefer we not share your name and address, please check here. ☐

SSE09R

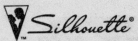
Silhouette®

COMING NEXT MONTH
Available May 26, 2009

#1975 A BRAVO'S HONOR—Christine Rimmer
Bravo Family Ties
For more than a century, battling ranch families the Bravos and the
Cabreras made the Hatfield and McCoy feud look like child's play.
Until Mercy Cabrera fell for Luke Bravo, and their forbidden love
tested the very limits of a Bravo's honor.

#1976 A FORTUNE WEDDING—Kristin Hardy
Fortunes of Texas: Return to Red Rock
It had been nearly twenty years since the one-night fling between
Frannie Fortune and Roberto Mendoza. But now Roberto was back,
and secrets of their past exploded into the present—along with an
ironclad love that could not be denied.

#1977 LOVING THE RIGHT BROTHER—Marie Ferrarella
Famous Families
When tragedy struck, Irena Yovich headed back to Hades, Alaska,
to console her ex-boyfriend's family—and began seeing his brother
Brody Hayes, her best friend from high school, in a very different
light. Things were really about to heat up in Hades….

#1978 LEXY'S LITTLE MATCHMAKER—Lynda Sandoval
Return to Troublesome Gulch
When the desperate boy called nine-one-one, little did EMS
dispatcher Lexy Cabrera know that the little hero's father,
Drew Kimball, whose life they saved that day, would turn around and
heal *her*…with a love she'd all but given up on finding!

#1979 THE TYCOON'S PERFECT MATCH—Christine Wenger
The Hawkins Legacy
Brian Hawkins and Marigold Sherwood had spent summers at
Hawk's Lake loving each other—until Mari moved away and a
misunderstanding tore them apart. Now that CEO Mari was back
in town, would all the old feelings come home to roost?

#1980 THE COWBOY'S SECOND CHANCE—Christyne Butler
Fate had not been kind to cowboy Landon Cartwright—loss and
shame dogged his every step. But then he walked right into the arms
of rancher and single mom Maggie Stevens…and a ray of light and
love reached the very darkest spots of his soul.

SSECNMBPA0509